I0775901

THE FEAR OF FIRE

Book Two in **THE FEAR OF** Series

S.C. Sterling

N/B Books

Book Design by Charles Layton

Ways to connect with Scott:
www.scsterling.com
sc@scsterling.com

ISBN: 979-8-9897265-1-6

In memory of Tyler. Thank you for being by my side
for eighteen years.

THE FEAR
OF FIRE

ZERO

"Talk to you later butthead," Casey said, hanging up the phone.

Resting her feet on the coffee table, she stared out the patio door. It was snowing yet again. This was her third winter in Wyoming, and while she thought she'd become accustomed to them, she hadn't. They were as brutal as everyone said, probably even worse. She couldn't decide what she hated more—the cold, the snow, or the wind. Probably the wind—that was year-round.

Growing up, she'd always loved winter—it was her favorite season—but as she got older, she began detesting the cold weather and the snow. More and more, she daydreamed of moving to Arizona or Florida after graduation. Life in Laramie was temporary.

Leaning back into the couch, she closed her eyes, but just as she started to doze off, the phone rang. Inching one eye open, she glared. It finally stopped in the middle of the seventh ring.

It was probably her best friend Robin, calling to ask her to go to the Cowboy Lounge, and when Casey said no, it'd eventually turn into begging. That was their usual Friday night drinking location, and there was a guy Robin wanted to introduce Casey to, but she didn't feel like being social.

All she really wanted was a Frosty and fries, but she was too tired to throw on a coat and drive the five blocks to Wendy's, so her night was going to consist of a long, hot shower, a frozen pepperoni pizza, and watching *Beetlejuice* on her worn-out VHS tape for probably the fiftieth time.

A little after eight, Casey placed the pizza in the oven, set the timer, then went into the bathroom and turned on the water and slipped off her clothes. Within a minute, steam filled the room and the mirror was covered with a layer of condensation. Casey preferred her showers with nearly scalding water, the hotter the better.

As she was washing her hair, a loud bang startled her—it sounded like it was coming from the patio. Then another one, this time louder. Something, or someone, had crashed into her sliding glass door.

Pulling open the curtain, Casey stuck her head out. "Hello? Is somebody there?" Her voice barely rose above the sound of the water.

Through the half-open door, Casey watched the hallway and a portion of the living room. The noise gave her an uneasy feeling. She turned off the water. Then, with suds still in her hair, she grabbed a towel and stepped out of the bathtub.

"If someone is out there, I have a gun and I know how to use it," she said, volume rising as she spoke.

That was a lie. She'd never even held a gun, let alone fired one. The closest form of protection in her apartment was her mismatched cutlery, but that was in the kitchen. If someone was in her apartment, her best line of defense would be screaming at the top of her lungs.

For about a minute, she stared into the living room. Nothing. She waited for about another twenty seconds, then scurried to the front door and checked the doorknob and deadbolt. They were both locked. Then she checked the patio door—also locked.

Standing in the middle of the living room, Casey stared at the kitchen wall, concluding that the noises had probably actually come from her neighbor Kyle, a gas station attendant who smoked enough marijuana for three people. As she walked back to the bathroom, she turned on the lights in the kitchen and hallway.

After finishing her shower, she ate half the pizza, accompanied by a beer, and then inserted the tape into the VCR. She curled onto the couch, and within ten minutes she was drifting to sleep. Later in the night, she awoke to static on the TV screen. Barely awake, she turned it off and made her way into the bedroom, then crawled under the comforter and closed her eyes.

Something woke her, and instantly she sensed that someone was in her room, next to her bed. Casey prayed that it was a dream, a nightmare. Slowly, she opened her eyes and saw the silhouette of a man hovering over her. He was donned in all black. Black pants, black hoodie, black gloves, and a black ski mask. Through the opening of the ski mask, she could see the whites of his eyes. Just as she was about to scream, he pressed the edge of a cold knife against her throat.

"If you scream, I'll slice your fucking throat from ear to ear," he whispered.

Casey didn't recognize the voice, but he sounded older—definitely not a college student. Fear rushed through her body. This could not be happening to her. Not her.

Paralyzed, she faintly muttered, "Who are you?"

The man stood still for a long moment, then shook his head.

"What do you want?" she said, her voice quivering.

Again, he shook his head in a steady motion, remaining silent. Without him taking his eyes off Casey, the blade started inching down her neck, stopping at the crest of her sternum. Casey glanced down at the knife, then back up at the man.

As much as she wanted to cry, she didn't want to appear weak. And as much as she wanted to fight, she knew her only option at the moment was to comply with his demands, no matter how vile they might be. She'd wait for an opening to grab the knife or run out the front door. And if he forced oral on her, she'd bite down as hard as she could.

Searching for something to say, she blurted, "I have herpes. I do. I don't have a breakout right now, but if you fuck me, you'll get herpes, I promise."

That was another lie. She remembered reading a news story about a girl who'd said the same thing during an attack, and the man had released the girl without harming her. She prayed that this man would believe her and leave the apartment.

"Yeah, like you have a gun?" His voice was ice cold.

Shivers ran through her entire body. It'd been hours since she yelled that. He must've been watching her the entire night. She tried to think of a response, but her mind was blank.

"This'll all be over soon," he said.

Out of the corner of her eye, Casey saw a fist coming down on her. There was no time to react, so she turned her head and closed her eyes. In a fraction of a second, everything went black.

When she regained consciousness, her vision was blurry and her head was throbbing. The mattress was wet under her. Either blood or urine, maybe both. Her sense of time had vanished; she had no idea how long she'd been knocked out or if the man was still in her apartment.

Glancing down, she saw that her pajama top had been ripped open, and her breasts were exposed. The bedsheet covered her below the waist, but she assumed her bottoms had been torn off as well. Her lips were bound with duct tape, same with her wrists and ankles. She knew she'd been raped, but she didn't want to think about it. All she wanted was for the man to be gone.

The room was empty—no sign of him. Closing her eyes, she leaned toward the hallway and listened. The apartment was still. Silent. Ten seconds, nothing. Twenty seconds. Thirty. Nothing. After what felt like minutes of complete silence, she was certain the man was no longer in her apartment.

She attempted to scream, but her voice was muted. Another attempt, this time with every remaining ounce of strength to open her mouth, but her jaw barely moved and the scream was only audible to her. For a fleeting second, she thought she was going to vomit, but she managed to fight the urge. With her taped mouth, it could lead to death by aspiration.

Unable to scream, Casey knew no one could help her. She was alone. Completely alone.

Turning away, she stared at the courtyard light shining through the blinds and started cursing herself. If she'd only met Robin at the bar, the man would have found no one home and probably searched for another victim. She might have gotten drunk and stayed at Robin's apartment, or maybe she would've run into Jack, her ex-boyfriend, at one of the campus bars and gone home with him. Or maybe she would've gone home with another guy. Countless seemingly inconsequential events that could've changed the outcome of her life forever.

Then her thoughts shifted to Hannah. Thankfully, the blizzard had happened when it did, because if it had been a few days earlier or later, Hannah would've come up for the weekend like they'd planned. She would've been sleeping on the couch when the man entered the apartment, and she'd most likely be a victim by now. At least Casey didn't have to live her final moments knowing that. Better her than Hannah.

Just as she was about to attempt to roll out of bed, the toilet flushed and the faucet turned on. Casey forced her eyes closed, not wanting him to see that she'd regained consciousness.

Never a religious person, she nonetheless started to pray, a final hope to be saved. She prayed that a neighbor had seen the man break into her apartment and had called the police. She prayed a friend would show up unannounced, scaring the man away. She prayed the man would leave the apartment and never return. But she was certain none of her prayers would be answered.

The man crept into the room and stopped at the edge of the bed. There was a faint smell of cheap cologne, something a middle-aged divorcee would wear. As he hovered over her, he started humming a song, and at first Casey attempted to ignore it, but he grew louder and louder, and it became impossible. It took a moment to place the song, but finally she recognized it as "Cherry Cherry" by Neil Diamond.

Then, starting at her belly button, he slowly ran his finger up her stomach, over her breasts, and up her chin, where he began circling her lips.

"Look at me," he said, tapping lightly on her cheek. "I know you can hear me."

Casey didn't want to look into the eyes of the man who was going to kill her. After a second of silence, he leaned into her face, holding the knife under her chin once more.

"I said, look at me."

Casey turned, and their eyes met. Almost instantly, she looked away.

"What is this?" he said, lifting Casey's silver flower pendant necklace off her chest.

"No, no," she muttered through the tape, her eyes becoming wet.

"I'm sorry, but you have no choice in the matter."

Gripped by a paralyzing fear, she said, "Please don't kill me."

The man smiled, then ripped the necklace off and slipped it into his pocket. Then, without saying a word, he plunged the knife into her upper abdomen. She cried out and attempted to squirm, but with his other hand, the man positioned his rough fingers around her neck, beginning to squeeze the life out of her.

As she lay motionless on the bed, bleeding out, he stabbed her two more times, then with the knife still in her flesh, he twisted the blade to the left, then to the right, and back to the left.

Blood began cascading down the sides of her stomach, drowning the mattress. The pain was overwhelming, and in a final attempt for help, Casey screamed, but the cry was only heard by her and the man.

Just as she was about to black out, as if he knew the exact moment, the man released his grasp around her neck and removed the knife, then took a few steps back. He lit a cigarette and admired his work, like a painter admiring their masterpiece.

When he was finished, he dropped the cigarette onto the carpet, stomped it out with his boot, then picked up the butt and slipped it into his pocket. Then he backed out of the bedroom and disappeared into the hallway. Moments later, Casey heard the patio door open, then close. The man was gone, and she was alone.

With her remaining strength, she began rocking back and forth in an attempt to sit up, but she couldn't. She was too weak. It felt like every heart beat was becoming fainter and further apart. The tape over her mouth made her feel like she was suffocating, a ship at the bottom of the sea, running out of air.

Any chance of survival was rapidly fading, and there was no question in her mind she was dying. Without a miracle, she'd be dead within hours. Her life over, before it even started, not even twenty-one.

Minutes passed like seconds, and hours passed like minutes. Sometime that morning, the sun shone down through the blinds, and she could hear voices in the courtyard and cars leaving the parking lot. People were going on about their day, going to work, going to school, going to get coffee.

Suddenly, everything she'd never experience again started running through her head. She'd never see another sunset. She'd never go on another hike. She'd never hear the laughter of another person, never have another kiss. She would never put her feet in the ocean—and she'd never hear Hannah's voice again.

In those final moments, all Casey could think about was Hannah. She wanted to tell her that she loved her, and that she was an amazing sister and friend, and that she was going to miss her. All she wanted was to see Hannah one last time, to hug and hold her.

Turning to the blinds, she stared at the sunlight for a moment. Then, with no more strength to keep her eyes open, they slowly started to close.

ONE

About a dozen pronghorn grazed in the open field across the highway from the Motel 6. Hannah leaned against the railing and watched them for a long time, occasionally taking a drag off a cigarette. There wasn't a soul in sight, just her and the pronghorn. She couldn't remember the last time she'd seen an animal in the wild—well, besides the occasional stray cat in a downtown Denver alley. It was tranquil, almost like she was watching an old-time Western.

Her alarm was set for seven thirty, but after tossing and turning all night, she'd finally decided to crawl out of bed a little after six. Like a kid on Christmas morning, she was excited for what the days and weeks would bring. She was also terrified that she'd find nothing and have to go back to Denver with her tail between her legs, no closer to solving Casey's murder.

After about five minutes, the pronghorn disappeared into the horizon and the rising sun. Even with the daybreak, the morning was frigid, probably only in the low twenties.

Despite it being the second week in November, it felt like the middle of winter. Initially, her plan was to arrive in July or August to avoid the harsh weather, but temporarily closing the PI firm had taken longer than she'd expected.

After taking the final drag, Hannah dropped the cigarette butt, then stomped it into the second-floor walkway and turned back to her door. She stared at the room number: 224. All even numbers that, if multiplied, totaled sixteen, her second favorite number. A good omen.

Side-stepping a crack in the walkway, she entered the room, then fastened the chain. Lumpy queen bed, cheap fake wood nightstand and dresser, TV with tin foil wrapped around the antenna, and yellow, smoke-stained ceiling. It wasn't a five-star hotel, it wasn't even three stars, but it didn't matter—it was a place to lay her head and sleep. The plan was to be here for a few weeks, maybe a month tops, then never, ever come back to Laramie or Wyoming.

In the bathroom, she locked the door, turned on the shower, and waited three minutes until the water was hot. After the quick rinse, she barely dried herself, pulling her hair back and slipping on some clothes. Sitting on the edge of the bed, she opened the nightstand drawer and removed her gun from where it lay next to the Bible.

Hannah made her way to the front lobby, where a lady, probably in her sixties, was complaining about a clogged toilet. The front desk clerk looked annoyed. After he gave multiple reassurances that maintenance would fix it within the hour, the lady stormed out, mumbling obscenities.

Approaching the counter, Hannah greeted the clerk.

"How can I help you this morning?" he said.

"I was wondering where I could grab some breakfast. Just looking for something simple, eggs and coffee."

"Well, my favorite spot is Annie's Diner. You're not going

to find a better meal for a better deal in town. I personally love the French toast."

"That sounds lovely. Could you give me directions?"

The clerk looked up at Hannah and smiled. Then he grabbed a pen and started drawing a map of Laramie on a piece of motel stationery.

She drove the half mile to the diner and was soon seated at the countertop. A man wearing overalls, probably a farmer or mechanic, sat two stools to her left, while the two stools to her right were empty. She ordered a coffee and the Sunrise Special, which consisted of two scrambled eggs, two slices of bacon, hash browns, and an English muffin.

As she ate, she skimmed the *Fort Collins Coloradoan*. On page seven, a headline caught her eye: "Drunk Driver Dies in Single-Car Accident Outside of Wellington." In the third sentence, the article listed the name of the driver: Cory Baker. That was a name Hannah hadn't heard in a long time, and she instantly became nauseous.

Hannah and Cory had worked together at a Blockbuster Video in Fort Collins. At the time, she was barely sixteen and a sophomore—it was the first real job she'd ever had. Cory was two years older and a senior at a different high school.

After their first shift together, Hannah had developed a crush on him. Tall, with deep blue eyes, a perfect smile, and the funniest person she knew. But she'd seen his girlfriend and knew she'd never stand a chance with him. The other girl was beautiful and popular, and she came from a perfect family, her dad being the mayor of Fort Collins. Hannah, meanwhile, considered herself awkward, average looking at best, and her family was the definition of dysfunctional.

That didn't stop him from flirting with her every time they worked together, and that didn't stop her from daydreaming about them being a couple.

About three months after she started, they had a Saturday night closing shift together. After the last customer left and the doors were locked, he unzipped his backpack and pulled out a bottle of whiskey and a two-liter of Coke. He poured two drinks, offering her one. Without hesitation, Hannah grabbed the cup and took a large swig. She'd drank before and been drunk more times than she could count, but it was almost always alone, pouring vodka from her dad's bottle and then refilling it with water.

Before they left the store that night, Cory invited her back to his house to drink some more. She declined at first, saying that she didn't think it was a good idea. Up to that point, she'd only kissed two boys, and no one she was romantically interested in had seen her naked. But Cory was persistent, and she finally caved and agreed to go.

That night, she lost her virginity. And the next morning, he barely said a word to her before kicking her out, using the excuse that his parents would be home soon and she couldn't be there when they arrived. When she said goodbye, she tried to kiss him, but he turned away. Being young and naive, she daydreamed that he'd break up with his girlfriend and they'd start a relationship.

For the first time since Casey had been murdered, Hannah was happy—she felt like a normal teenager. And for the first time in her life, she felt like she was falling in love. Yet her calls to him went unanswered and unreturned, and the five or six times she drove by his house, his car was never in the driveway.

Their next shift together was a week after they had sex. That entire day, she rehearsed exactly how she'd act and exactly what she'd say, obsessing over the color of eyeshadow to wear and practicing her smile in the mirror, over and over and over again.

After pulling into a parking spot, she spit her gum

into the ashtray, applied cherry-red lipstick—her favorite color—and smiled in the rearview mirror one final time. Then she stepped out of her car and skipped across the parking lot and into the store.

The moment she saw Cory, she ran up and attempted to hug him, but he kept his distance, barely acknowledging her. Throughout the shift, he ignored her every time she tried to talk to him, always escaping to the back room or outside for a cigarette.

Finally, she cornered him near the New Release section. "Are you mad at me?" The words rushed out.

"Just been really busy."

"Umm, it feels like you're trying to ignore me or something."

"No," he said, shaking his head, avoiding eye contact.

"Okay," Hannah said uncertainly. After a gaping pause, she said, "I was wondering if you wanted to hang out tonight, if you don't have any plans."

"I can't."

"Well, maybe we could do something next weekend then, possibly?"

His eyes eventually settled on her, and she knew what he was going to say before he spoke.

"Listen, you're a nice girl, but the other night was a mistake."

Her legs went weak. "A mistake? You told me you liked me."

"I was fucking wasted. I'm sure I said a lot of dumb shit."

Her heart was slowly breaking. "But I thought we were going to be together."

A smirk formed. "You really thought I was going to break up with Jackie to be with you? I was drunk, okay. We fucked, and that's it. Nothing more. And I can promise it'll never happen again."

Unable to speak, Hannah watched Cory walk away, tears blurring her vision. Before he was out of view, she cursed him under her breath, then turned away and fled from the store, never to return or speak to Cory again.

On the drive home that day, Hannah had become numb, and much like being blackout drunk, she couldn't remember the walk to her car, or stopping at intersections, or putting on her pajamas or grabbing the razor blade and resting it against her right wrist.

It wasn't that Hannah was suicidal—she just wanted the pain to stop. The pain over how she'd lost her virginity in a drunken stupor, the pain of falling for someone who'd only used her for sex, the pain of never being able to see or talk to Casey again, the pain of her survivor's guilt, knowing she should have been on the couch when the killer entered the apartment, the pain that her parents were broken beyond repair, her dad a full-blown alcoholic and her mother distant and detached, and the pain that she might never be as close to anyone again as she had been with Casey—she very well might be alone for the rest of her life. The thought of the blade slicing her flesh felt like an escape from all that pain. Over the next hour, she ran it up and down her arm, finally crying herself asleep.

She hadn't thought about Cory or that night in a very long time, and seeing his name in the newspaper stirred up the hatred that had settled in her when she was sixteen. She felt pathetic that it still lingered. *Would it ever truly go away?* Probably not, some scars never fully heal.

For a fleeting moment, Hannah smiled, joyous that he was dead, but that quickly shifted to guilt. As much as she reviled him, she'd never wished ill on him, and she became queasy that the thought of someone being dead brought a smile to her face. She placed her fork on the plate and stared at the half-eaten piece of bacon, feeling uneasy.

As the waitress walked by, Hannah looked up and said, "Excuse me, could you tell me where the nearest floral shop is?"

"Please, call me Nancy. And yes, swing a left out that door then left on third, then it's like five or six blocks up. Can't miss it."

"Thank you."

Nancy smiled and took three steps toward the kitchen, then abruptly stopped and walked back to the counter. "Wait a second, I knew I recognized your face from somewhere. You're that girl that solved the Megan Floyd murder, right?"

Hannah offered a slight nod, then looked away, her face turning red.

"What is your name?" Nancy said.

"Hannah Jacobs."

"That's right. I bawled my eyes out watching that story. You did amazing work. And you gave hope to some people in these parts who have missing loved ones that those cases might be solved."

Hannah had conducted one interview with Channel 4 in Denver, and she always regretted it at moments like this. She had never been one for accolades.

"Thank you so much, but I couldn't have solved it without my partner."

Nancy stared down at Hannah for a few more seconds. "Give me the check. Breakfast is on me."

"No, no. I insist on paying."

The woman slid the plate to the side and leaned on the counter, looking Hannah directly in the eyes.

"Can I tell you a story, Hannah?" Without waiting for a response, she continued talking. "My sister, Kelly, was in an abusive relationship for almost a decade. The piece of shit would come home from work, get drunk, then proceed to beat the living shit out of her. And then say how sorry he was and that he loved her and would never lay another hand on her again.

Like clockwork, this happened almost every weekend for the better part of their relationship. He put her in the hospital three times—a broken arm, three broken ribs, and a shattered eye socket. Hell, she was so good with her makeup that you could barely notice her black eyes.

I don't know how many times she called the cops, but they didn't do shit. Never. He'd say she was clumsy and tripped over something, or that she was drunk, or he'd make up some damn lie that he'd tell them. And those fucking cowards believed that bastard every single time."

The woman paused and glanced up, then took a deep breath. "Finally, with no other options, scared for her life, she summoned the strength and skipped town while he was at work. Two days later, he found her in a motel outside of Casper and put two bullets in her chest."

"I'm so sorry," Hannah murmured, barely audible even to her own ears.

Nancy swallowed hard, then rested her hands on top of Hannah's. "Please, as a token of my appreciation for finding that piece-of-shit woman killer, let me buy you breakfast. It's the least I can do, honey."

"Of course, thank you so much."

"No, thank you, sweetie. And be safe out there. This town doesn't seem dangerous, but looks are deceiving. There are a lot of men living here in sheep's clothing."

Nancy smiled, knocked on the counter twice, and then walked away.

When she disappeared into the kitchen, Hannah placed a twenty under the coffee cup before slipping out of the diner.

On the sidewalk in downtown Laramie, the morning

was quiet, the only sounds coming from vehicles on I-80 two miles to the east. The stillness made Hannah uncomfortable. She was used to the sounds of Denver: truck engines, car horns, dogs barking, and drug addicts screaming at the top of their lungs. The chaos of the city eased her demons. In the quiet, it was far too easy to get lost in her thoughts.

It took her about five minutes to get to the flower shop, and after browsing the display, Hannah selected the "In Loving Memory" arrangement, which had an assortment of white roses, white cremones, lilies, and snapdragons. She requested the bouquet be delivered to the funeral home in Fort Collins on the day of Cory's funeral.

"What would you like the card to say?"

Hannah gave the florist a blank stare; she hadn't considered the question. "Umm, how about, 'Please accept my deepest condolences.'"

"That's lovely," the florist said.

On the walk back to the car, Hannah stepped into Bart's House of Music, where she began thumbing through CD bins. After about ten bins, the man behind the counter said, "Can I help you find something, sweetie?"

She looked up, taking in his disheveled beard. "Honestly, I have no idea what I'm looking for. Do you offer recommendations?"

"Does a bear shit in the woods?"

Hannah grinned. Her dad had said that for as long as she could remember, and it always filled her with joy.

"Give me something in the vein of Radiohead."

The man started stroking his beard. "Ever heard of a band called Muse?"

Hannah shook her head slowly. "Can't say I have."

"Three-piece out of England. They just released their debut back in September. A lot of critics have been comparing it to *The Bends*."

"Really? That's my favorite album of all time, so if it's half as good as that, I'm sure I'll love it."

"I'll tell you what, if you buy it and don't like it, you can bring it back and exchange it for any other CD in the store."

"Deal."

After leaving Bart's House of Music, Hannah walked back to her car, then drove across town to the Sage Creek apartments. She reversed into a parking spot directly in front of the leasing office.

Hannah remained in her car for a solid twenty minutes, studying the office and the surrounding buildings and courtyard. The residents were a mixture of college students, parents in their late teens or early twenties, and retirees. A strange combination, but housing in Laramie was limited, and the complex catered to the low-income.

The buildings were canary yellow, a different color than she remembered, probably part of the rebranding effort after the murder. Just like the renaming of the complex, and the new landscaping, and the repaving of the parking lot. Nothing like a new, pretty sign and a fresh coat of paint to mask a brutal unsolved murder on the property.

Hannah walked across the parking lot and onto the pathway between two buildings, then past the swimming pool, a route she'd followed slews of times before. She could almost navigate it with her eyes closed. The closer she got to the apartment, the more she wanted to turn around, but she continued, though with slower and shorter strides.

Then, across the courtyard, she saw the patio of Casey's apartment. She stared at it for a long while, maybe two minutes, maybe five. The last time she'd seen her sister was on that patio. Casey was waving to Hannah and yelling goodbye as Hannah left to return home to Fort Collins. That memory was heartfelt, but it soon faded.

As she approached the patio, the glare from the sun diminished, and gradually she could see inside the apartment through the open blinds. There was no furniture in the living room or kitchen; all the doors were open, and all the lights were on. A sense of relief washed over Hannah as she realized the apartment was unoccupied.

As much as she wanted to see inside, she would've felt guilty lying to the tenants, and she wasn't about to tell someone about the horrible event that had occurred in the same room where they slept. Lying to a leasing agent, on the other hand, would never bother her—it was a requirement for the job.

Just then, a couple kids ran across the grass laughing, startling Hannah. She glanced over her shoulder and watched them until they disappeared around a building. Then she started across the courtyard to the leasing office.

A girl not much bigger than her, probably no older than twenty-two, looked up from the computer screen as Hannah walked in. After a quick introduction, Hannah sat down across from the girl. Her name was Rachel, and she smelled of Juicy Fruit.

"How can I help you today?" Rachel said.

"I was wondering if I could see an apartment."

"Are you looking for a one or two-bedroom?"

"I'm actually interested in seeing a specific apartment."

The girl looked sideways at Hannah for a moment, then whispered, "101 in building five?"

Hannah nodded. "I just took a peek, and it looks empty."

"It is, and it has been since that *Dateline* episode aired.

The tenants who were living in it demanded to move apartments, and we haven't been able to rent it since. It's been vacant for almost two years," Rachel said.

"Well, at least it probably makes the job interesting."

Rachel nodded feverishly. "Oh, it definitely does. And if I'm being honest, I've kinda become obsessed with the murder. I've probably been in that apartment at least two dozen times." The girl blew a bubble. "And I heard this rumor that someone is in town writing a true crime book. You know like in the style of *In Cold Blood*. I sure hope it's true—this town could use some excitement."

Hannah had never understood the fascination with true crime and murder. It sickened her that people got pleasure out of seeing the darkest, final days and moments of someone's life. Apparently, one person's tragedy could be another's entertainment.

"Do you think you could let me in for like ten minutes? I promise I'll be in and out."

After a short pause, Rachel said, "Wait a second. Are you the one writing the book?"

Hannah considered the question, then leaned in and whispered, "Can you keep a secret?"

Rachel leaned over the desk as well and spoke at an even softer level. "Yes, yes. Of course. I pinky swear I won't tell a soul."

"I'm doing the preliminary research for a book that is scheduled to be published late next year."

"Oh my God, that is so cool. If I let you take a look around, would you mention my name in the book?"

"Of course," Hannah said, forcing a smile.

Rachel opened a drawer, grabbed a set of keys, and offered Hannah a business card.

"And here's my card—it's got my home and work number. Feel free to call me anytime," she said with a wink.

Standing at the apartment door, Hannah could feel her pulse racing and her palms getting sweaty. She closed her eyes and could see the yellow crime scene tape still hanging across the door.

It'd felt like a lifetime since she'd stepped foot in the apartment. Ten days after the murder and three days after the funeral, Hannah and her dad had driven up to Laramie to pack Casey's belongings. At first, he'd vehemently objected to her joining, but Hannah insisted, knowing he didn't have the strength to do it alone.

As they walked past the living room down the hallway, the smell of iron became unbearable, and for a moment, she thought she was going to vomit. When they entered the bedroom, the mattress was leaning against the wall, soaked from head to foot with dark red blood, a color reminiscent of horror movies.

"They told me they got rid of the mattress," her dad whispered.

For the next seven hours, there was little conversation as they packed almost every last possession Casey owned, placing it in the back of a ten-foot U-Haul. Clothes, shoes, books, pictures, CDs, knickknacks, makeup, kitchen items, the coffee table and kitchen table and chairs. The only items that didn't go into the U-Haul were the mattress and couch. Those, they dropped next to the dumpster after dark.

Unlike the funeral, packing Casey's life into cardboard boxes was something Hannah hadn't been prepared for, and even a decade later, she wished she could forget.

"Go on in," Rachel said, gesturing into the apartment.

Hesitant, Hannah placed her left foot on the carpet, then her right. Rachel said something, but Hannah didn't comprehend it. White noise, in one ear and out the other.

The farther she walked into the apartment, the more

the memories became alive. Casey teaching Hannah to shotgun a beer, watching movies and laughing so much their stomachs hurt, seeing who could eat the most pizza in one sitting, and lying in the courtyard and staring up at the stars. Casey had taken an astronomy course in college, and could identify almost every constellation in the night sky. With each one, she'd grab Hannah's hand and trace the pattern over and over while slowly pronouncing each name.

"There's Pegasus, the winged horse. Oh, and there's Ursa Major, also known as Great Bear—or the Big Dipper."

As much as it pained her to return, Hannah had always known she'd start her investigation in the apartment. And it wasn't about finding new or undiscovered clues; the chances of that were zero. It was about reconnecting with Casey and the murder.

Methodically, Hannah made her way down the hallway, then stepped foot in the bedroom and leaned against the door frame. She looked over the room, which was going in and out of focus. Visions of carrying the blood-soaked mattress infiltrated her thoughts. The misery of that day had never faded, not one bit.

Finally, she turned back to Rachel. "Do you know if anyone still lives in this building from when Casey lived here?"

"No, not anymore."

"Anymore?" Hannah said, eyebrows raised.

"Well, Ms. Dorothy Bennett lived directly upstairs for almost twenty-one years, but she had a bad fall last year, so her family moved her into an assisted living facility. I think she was damn near eighty."

"And you think they lived in this building at the same time?"

"I'm positive they did. We had a little celebration for her twenty-year anniversary at the complex. Cake and soda, you know? And she told me she'd been here since 1978, in the same apartment. She seemed pretty proud of it, but I don't know why anyone would be proud of living here that long."

"Do you know where she moved?"

"Yeah. Gables Nursing Home. I had to forward her mail like once a month for a while," Rachel said, nodding.

"Is it in town?" Hannah said, pointing to the ground.

"Oh yeah, about ten minutes away."

A name of someone who might've been upstairs the night of the murder. She might've heard something or seen someone. Or she could have dementia and not even remember her own name. Still, it was a lead, and it was more than Hannah had when she woke up.

Cutting Rachel off mid-sentence, she made an excuse about having to be back at the hotel in twenty minutes for a call with her publisher. Graciously, she thanked Rachel for her time and started to the front door.

"Of course. And Hannah, if you have any more questions or want to see this place again, or just want any juicy gossip about people in this town, I'm the girl to call. Remember, my number is on the card, so please don't hesitate to give me a ring."

Glancing over her shoulder, Hannah offered a fleeting smile and then continued to the door.

At the first gas station, Hannah stopped next to a payphone then frantically started flipping pages in the phone book until she found the number to the nursing home. She pulled two quarters out of her pocket then dialed and leaned into the phone booth, waiting for someone to answer.

On the third ring, she hung up. Odds were they wouldn't allow unsolicited calls to residents for safety reasons, and on the off chance they did transfer to Dorothy's room,

Hannah knew she couldn't convey the reason for the call.

You don't know me, but you lived above my sister who was murdered a decade ago, and I'm calling to see if you remember anything about that night.

No, this conversation would have to be done in person. Hannah grabbed the quarters out of the change return and began flipping a coin while walking back to her car.

On the drive to Gables Nursing Home, she deliberated how she could enter the building, get past the check-in desk, and avoid the security guards—as well as probably another half dozen employees—and then find and enter Dorothy's room.

Lying would be difficult, if not impossible. Nursing homes usually required an ID, and that name had to match one on the approved visitor list. She considered herself an excellent liar, but pleading that she was the woman's granddaughter probably wouldn't get her past the lobby.

The next idea was to sneak in through an unlocked door. The chances of a maintenance or cafeteria or janitorial worker forgetting to lock a door were high, and that would give her access to the building, but finding the correct room while staying undetected after would be a tall order. The building could have fifty or a hundred rooms, and probably with no nameplates on the doors. She'd need access to the directory.

Then it hit her—she could impersonate an employee.

Once she arrived, Hannah watched the nursing home and parking lot from across the street for almost an hour. Activity was minimal. About half a dozen residents on walks, a nurse pushing someone in a wheelchair, and two other nurses or orderlies smoking on the side of the building. After the cigarette, one went back into the building while the other walked out into the parking lot, retrieved something from a car, and then headed back in as well.

Hannah kept her attention on the parking lot. It was on the south side of the building, out of view from the main entrance. Seven cars were spread out across the lot, all of them probably belonging to employees.

A little after twilight, Hannah grabbed her backpack, crossed the street, and made her way into the lot. She strolled by the cars, inspecting each one, searching for a pair of scrubs, an embroidered polo shirt, an apron. Anything that would give her the right appearance.

In the third car, she found a pair of scrubs folded neatly on the backseat. Unzipping her backpack, she removed a Slim Jim, popped the lock, opened the door enough to grab the scrubs, tossed everything in her backpack, and started back to her car. It had taken less than thirty seconds to break into the car, and she was in the parking lot for less than three minutes total. She was confident that nobody had seen her, and that no one would know she'd been there.

After driving about ten blocks north, she parked in the back of an apartment complex between two minivans. She scanned the lot, the building, the street, and the alley. It seemed like a good location to hide her car for a few hours.

Reaching down to the passenger floor, she grabbed her backpack and removed the scrubs, placing them on the steering wheel. Excitement instantly faded when she saw the "XL" printed on the tag.

"Fuck," she said, shaking her head.

The scrub top could almost double as a dress on Hannah, and even after putting it on over her shirt and tucking it deep into her jeans, there was still about six inches of garment hanging below her waist. It'd have to do. She didn't even bother with the bottoms.

Back at the nursing home, Hannah studied the building again for almost ten minutes. Not a single person entered or exited, though two cars had left since she was in the parking lot earlier. The day shift was over, and the night shift was on. Most likely a skeleton crew. And generally, night shift and graveyard workers didn't have a high regard for their employer compared to day shift workers, so getting into the building and finding Dorothy should be easier in the evening than in the morning or midday.

Hannah started preparing herself mentally. In theory, the plan was simple—enter the building through an unlocked door then find a resident who could tell her Dorothy's room number, all while attempting to avoid any real staff members. And if she did run into an employee, she'd learned from a previous experience that the crucial key to not getting detected was to act like you belonged there. Don't avoid eye contact, but don't stare too long. Say hello, smile, then go on about your fucking business.

Glancing at her watch, she saw that it was a little after six. Dinner had probably just ended, and most residents were probably either in an activity area or in their rooms. The perfect time to sneak in.

Hannah made her way to the back of the building then up the pathway to a door. Carefully, she placed her fingers around the handle and pulled. It was locked. Hoping it needed a little extra force, she tried again. No luck.

"Strike one," she whispered.

The second door was also locked, but the third door opened. After looking back to the courtyard to make sure no one was watching, she opened it wide enough to slip inside, then eased it shut behind her.

Death was in the air. It reminded Hannah of visiting her grandma in hospice three days before she died. During that visit, Grandma had thought Hannah was a nurse and asked who she was about a dozen times, her eyes full of confusion. After she died, Hannah made a promise to herself that if she was ever diagnosed with dementia, she'd hike deep into the mountains, place a gun into her mouth, and pull the trigger.

The corridor was narrow and about fifteen feet from what she surmised was the main hallway. The only light came from an exit sign on the ceiling. Stepping back into the corner, she was confident that she was nearly invisible.

She tapped her thigh in a rapid rhythm, studying the residents walking past. She watched for about three minutes without seeing a single person in scrubs. That was a very good sign.

Hannah darted to the main hallway, and when the fluorescent lights hit her eyes, they momentarily blinded her. After a couple of frantic seconds of blinking, the blind spots faded and she saw a group of four women playing cards in a room across the hall.

"Excuse me, I was wondering if one of you could tell me what room Dorothy Bennett is in?"

They stared at each other and were speechless for so long that Hannah became certain they knew she was an impostor. Then one of them looked up at her and said, "Dorothy, I think she's in room 42." The rest of them nodded in agreement. "Yes, room 42," they said in near unison.

Hannah thanked them and scurried across the tile and up the hallway, keeping her head down. After passing two rooms, she realized she was going in the wrong direction. She turned around, and as she passed the group of women playing cards again, she smiled and nodded.

After making one more wrong turn, Hannah was standing in front of room number 42. It'd been less than five minutes since she entered the building, and to her surprise, she still hadn't seen a single employee.

She gave three soft knocks on the door, then waited

ten seconds, then knocked three more times.

A frail voice on the other side said, "Hello."

Hannah inched the door open and took a step into the room. "Ms. Bennett?"

The lady was perched on the edge of the bed, watching the local news. Almost in slow motion, she turned around and looked up at Hannah. "You're not Betty," she said with a touch of trepidation.

Hannah gave the door a gentle nudge to close it, then walked in and sat down next to Dorothy. She sensed the lady was moments from yelling for help. *Speak in a soft and comforting voice, and don't make any sudden movements.*

"Are you the Dorothy Bennett who lived at the Sage Creek apartments?"

"Yes, I lived in apartment 201 since 1978. I was forced to move here by my daughter after I slipped and broke my ankle."

Hannah nodded, keeping her face serene. "I was wondering if I could ask a couple questions about your time living there."

"I'll do my best, darling, but I turn eighty-two this year, and my memory isn't what it used to be."

"That's perfectly fine. Anything you remember will help immensely," Hannah said. She held up a picture of Casey. "I was wondering if you remember this girl."

The lady studied Hannah for a moment, then lowered her eyes to the picture. "Oh my gosh, I haven't seen that lovely face in such a long time."

"So, you remember her?"

"I do. What was her name? Kelly? Katie?"

"Casey."

"Yes, that's right. Bless her heart, bless her heart. It was such a tragedy what happened to her. I think the entire town was in shock for months. Years. I had friends who started locking their doors who had never locked their doors before. It scared a lot of people."

Hannah inched closer. "Ms. Bennett, I'm Casey's sister, Hannah. And I'm trying to solve her murder. I'm searching for any clues that could help me find the person who did it."

"Please, call me Dorothy," she said.

"Okay, Dorothy," Hannah said with a smile. "I know this happened over ten years ago, but do you remember if you saw anyone or heard anything out of the ordinary on the night of the murder? It was a Saturday—January 21, 1989, if that helps."

"I wasn't home when it happened."

"No?"

"No, I was in Europe with my sister. I think we left that Tuesday before it happened, and we were gone for almost four weeks. Would you like to see pictures?"

"Maybe another time." Hannah smiled again. "Before you left for Europe, do you remember seeing any suspicious people who seemed out of place? Like they didn't belong there?"

Dorothy intertwined her fingers and leaned back. "Well, about a week or two before my trip I do recall this man walking away from our building. There was something about him that gave me the heebie-jeebies. I thought he might've been trying to break into an apartment so I watched him all the way to the parking lot. He never looked back, just climbed into his truck and sped away so fast that he almost hit someone walking their dog."

"Did you happen to get a good look at him?"

"Kind of. He was white, average height, probably in his thirties, with a long, full beard. And he was wearing sunglasses. I thought that was strange because it was night outside."

"Did you ever see him again?"

"No," she said, shaking her head.

"Did you happen to see what kind of truck he was driving?"

"I think it was a black or blue Ford F-150."

"Did you ever give a statement to police about the man in the truck?"

"Oh no, I never talked to any police officers. When I got back home the apartment was empty, and then a neighbor told me what happened and I couldn't believe it."

Just as Hannah was about to ask another question, the door flung open. A nurse hovered in the doorway.

"Ma'am, who are you? What are you doing in this room?"

Hannah leaned in, kissed Dorothy on the forehead then whispered, "Thank you for everything." Standing up, she said, "I'm just an old friend who's leaving."

The nurse turned down the hallway. "Security, we have an unauthorized visitor in Room 42."

Hannah didn't want to explain why she'd broken into a car, stolen a pair of scrubs, then broken into a nursing home to question an elderly resident. She wanted to keep a low profile for as long as possible, and ending up in a police station would ruin any attempts at staying anonymous.

As she stepped away from the bed, she weighed her escape options.

First option: Try to lie her way out of the situation. Say she was an old family friend passing through town who just wanted to say hello. That might've worked if she was wearing street clothes, but there'd be no feasible way to explain the scrubs.

Second option: Escape through the window. But with it being a ground-floor room, there could be a locking mechanism that wouldn't allow someone, even someone of Hannah's size, to fit through the opening.

Third option, and in Hannah's opinion, the best and only viable one: Rush the nurse, and flee the building before security arrives. The nurse probably had about twenty pounds on her, but she'd be no match for an unexpected full-sprint shove.

"I can explain. Let me find my credentials," Hannah said, reaching into her pocket.

Then she sprinted toward the door, and with arms out, elbows locked, she shoved the nurse, making the woman fall hard onto the tile.

"I'm so sorry!" Hannah yelled.

As she sprinted down the hall, Hannah spotted a fire exit sign and ran straight toward it. Turning down a corridor, she barged through a door, then across the courtyard and across the parking lot and across the street, never looking back.

After four blocks, she slipped into an alley and crouched behind a restaurant dumpster. Once she caught her breath, she pulled off the scrub top and tossed it into the dumpster. Then she continued up the alley and was back to her car within minutes.

TWO

Five minutes after Wyoming Bell opened, Hannah entered the building and navigated the oddly positioned chairs in the lobby. An elderly lady who resembled Bea Arthur from the Golden Girls greeted Hannah as she approached the counter.

"I have somewhat of a strange request. I'm searching for a couple of friends from high school who I want to reconnect with, and all I have is their phone numbers, but both of them are disconnected," Hannah said, twirling her hair. "I was wondering if you could look up their names and numbers and see if they were transferred to a different number, or account, or anything like that."

She studied Hannah for what felt like forever, and for a moment Hannah thought the lady knew she was lying, but finally she said, "Give me the numbers, and I'll see what I can do."

There'd been about three dozen numbers in Casey's phone book, and all of them were either disconnected, or the person was no longer living at the residence. The only two names Hannah recognized were Jack Cunningham, Casey's ex-boyfriend, and Robin Davidson, Casey's best friend at the time of her murder. They were also the only two she wanted to speak with.

As the woman was typing, she said, "You're lucky, we just spent the last six months transferring all of our paper files into digital records, or else I wouldn't be able to help you."

"Lucky me," Hannah said with an exaggerated smile.

"Okay, it looks like Jack's number was canceled in '90 due to non-payment, no forwarding information, and Robin's number was transferred to Casper in '92, and then again to Evanston in '96. And that number and account is currently active."

"Could you give me her number and address?"

"Yes, let me print that out for you."

After thanking the lady, Hannah exited the building and jogged across the street to a payphone. She inserted two quarters into the coin slot, then dialed Robin's number. On the third ring, a woman answered.

"Are you Robin Davidson?"

"Yes, that's my maiden name. Who is this?"

"My name is Hannah, and I'm Casey Jacob's little sister. I was wondering if I could ask you a couple questions about her murder."

There was a long pause, long enough that Hannah thought the line might've gotten disconnected.

"Hello? Hello?" Hannah said.

"Yes, I'm here. It's just been a very long time since I've heard that name. And I didn't think anyone would ever ask me about her again. To this day I still haven't had a friend like her." She let out a sigh. "Have we ever met?"

"Yeah, I think maybe at the funeral, or the gathering after, or maybe both. I don't exactly recall—that day was kind of a blur."

"That's right. I remember you doing the eulogy. It was beautiful. Casey would've been proud."

Writing the eulogy was one of the toughest things Hannah had ever done, and would probably ever have to do. Barely a teenager, she'd never been to a funeral and wasn't sure what to say. Her older sister, her best friend, her mentor—everything in Hannah's world was dead, and she had no clue how to put to words the importance of Casey's life into a few measly paragraphs.

Hannah had stayed awake for nearly forty-eight hours prior to the funeral, writing and rewriting and editing the eulogy until she deemed it was perfect. And by the time of the funeral, she was in a dream state from sleep deprivation. During the eulogy, she kept her eyes glued on the paper, crippled by anxiety, but when she finished and looked up there wasn't a dry eye in the building.

"Thank you," Hannah murmured.

"Please, ask whatever questions you have," Robin said.

"In your police report, you stated you were with Jack the entire night of the murder?"

From day one, Jack had been the initial suspect, but on the night of the murder, he'd been at the Cowboy Lounge until closing, and after last call he went to an on-campus house party and passed out on the couch until sunrise. Nearly a dozen people, including Robin, had provided an alibi that from 2 a.m. until 8 a.m., he was on the couch. After Jack was cleared, there was never a viable suspect again.

"Yes, we closed down the bar, then went to our friend Frank's house, and Jack did a couple vodka shots. He was passed out within twenty minutes. I, on the other hand—and please don't repeat this—did a little blow and stayed up the entire night, and I swear on my life Jack never stepped foot off the couch, not even to use the bathroom. I distinctly remember talking to a friend about how drunk he was, and how he wasn't even bothered by the music. It was so loud I thought for sure he was going to wake up, but he never did." Robin let out a nervous laugh.

"How was he after it happened?"

"Sorry, can you hold on a second?"

"Sure."

"Be quiet! I'm on the damn phone. Go play your Nintendo and I'll be down there in a minute." Robin shouted through a muffled receiver. "Sorry about that—I can't get five minutes alone in my own house."

"It's fine."

"I love those kids more than anything, but they are a pain in my you-know-what. Sorry, what did you ask again?"

Hannah repeated the question.

"Oh, he was devastated, a complete shell of himself. When you talked to him, it was like he wasn't there. He blamed himself for what happened, like he should have been her protector or something. He told everyone that if they hadn't broken up, he would've been at her apartment and she'd still be alive."

"Do you know why they broke up?"

"Something dumb, I'm sure. They'd get in these drunken fights, break up, then get back together a few weeks later. I'd venture to say it happened at least ten times. They were the couple that annoyed the hell out of each other when they were together, but were miserable when they were apart."

"Are you still in contact with him?"

"No, it's been years. Last I heard, he was living somewhere down south, Arkansas or Mississippi."

"Do you know if she was seeing anyone else on one of their breaks? Or if there was someone else she was interested in?"

"I remember being asked this question by the investigator, and I said no at the time, but now, after all these years, I think there might've been something going on with one of our professors."

"Who?" Hannah said abruptly.

"Professor Reynolds. Gregory Reynolds," Robin said. "He was smart, funny, good-looking, and only about ten years older than us. I had a crush on him, and so did about half the girls in our class, but for Casey it seemed like more than a stupid crush. She talked about him all the time, and I saw them flirting on numerous occasions, and one day after class, I forgot my backpack and went back to get it, and when I walked into the room, they were standing right next to each other and they both looked at me and stared. It was really weird. You know that feeling you get when you walk into a room and someone is doing something they shouldn't be doing, and there's a guilty look on their face? Well, Casey and Gregory both had that look."

"Did you ever ask Casey if she was dating him?" Hannah said.

"Not directly, but I did tease her once, said something like the only reason she was getting an A was because they were sleeping together. I don't think I ever saw her that mad. She was furious."

"And you never told this to the police?"

"No, I was pretty much a kid, barely twenty when they questioned me. I was so dumb and naive about the situation, and I really didn't think anything wrong about it, but looking back now, as an adult with two kids, it definitely seemed inappropriate between a teacher and a student." She sighed. "Let's just say if I ever see my daughter and her teacher acting how they did, I'd punch him square in the nose."

In the back row of the auditorium, Hannah watched Professor Reynolds lecture a class of about 150 students. She was mesmerized by his ability to command the room like a conductor. Public speaking was foreign to her. She'd rather get the flu than have to speak in front of an audience of more than five people.

As he paced the lecture stage, Hannah could see how a young student could fall for him. He was charming and witty and exuded confidence—quite dashing. A silver fox, who'd probably only gotten better looking as he aged. Hannah had only been in the classroom for ten minutes, and just looking around she could see that some of the girls were smitten with him.

When the class was over, Hannah lowered her head and made her way down the aisle. The crowd filed out of the auditorium and into the hallway. Hannah began searching for a female student to ask for his contact information.

"Excuse me, I lost my syllabus and I need to speak to Professor Reynolds about an assignment. Would you happen to have his office number and hours?" Hannah said.

"Of course, let me grab it from my binder," the girl said.

After navigating a series of hallways and having to ask three more people, Hannah finally located the professor's office. Leaning against the wall, she watched the office door for almost twenty minutes. Nobody entered or left, and the door never opened. She prayed that he was in, and that he was alone.

Finally, she pushed off the wall and walked across the hallway. After knocking on the door, she waited. As she was about to knock again, it opened.

"Hello, how can I help you today?" Professor Reynolds

said with a welcoming smile.

"I was wondering if I could talk to you for a few minutes in private?"

The professor studied Hannah for a moment, looking her up and down. "Sure, come on in."

As Hannah entered the office, he ushered her to a chair in front of his desk, placing his hand on the small of her back as he guided her. The gesture made Hannah uncomfortable, but she didn't show it. Instead, she looked up at him and smiled.

After sitting down, he stared at her for a long stretch. "I'm sorry, but I don't recognize you. What is your name, and what class are you taking?"

"Well, that's because I'm not a student here."

"Oh," he said, eyebrows raised.

"My sister was, though. Casey Jacobs, do you remember her?"

"Yes, of course. She was a very bright student, and one of my favorites that year. What happened to her, and now Matthew, has rocked this town, and in some ways, I don't think it will ever recover." He paused, then shook his head. "I still can't believe Casey's murder hasn't been solved after all these years. How long has it been? Six? Eight years?"

"Ten."

"Wow, that long? Time really does fly the older you get," he said, then took a sip of water. "So, what can I help you with today?"

"Well, Professor Reynolds, I was wondering if I could ask you a couple of quick questions about Casey's time as a student here?"

"Please, call me Gregory."

"Nice to meet you, Gregory. I'm Hannah."

He smiled and nodded. "Well Hannah, I'd love to

help any way I can, but I highly doubt I can provide any pertinent information about the case."

"Anything you can remember will be helpful. Did you know her boyfriend, Jack Cunningham?"

"The name doesn't ring a bell, but it's been a long time, and I've probably had thousands of students between then and now."

Reaching across the desk, Hannah picked up a stress ball and balanced it in her palm. "She never mentioned him to you?"

"Not that I recall. But as a rule, I normally don't discuss personal relationships with my students."

"Did you ever see Casey outside of class?"

He started tapping a pen against the desk. Maybe it was nothing, or maybe it was a stall tactic, something to help him craft the perfect answers.

"No, I usually don't socialize with my students outside of the classroom," he said sarcastically.

"Usually? So, you do sometimes?"

"I meant to say, I don't have personal relationships with my students outside of academia, but this is a very small town, so on occasion, I will run into a student at the grocery store or gym or church."

Hannah placed the ball back on the desk. "Did you ever run into Casey at the grocery store or gym, or anywhere else outside of campus?"

"Not that I recall, Hannah," he said, his voice low.

Even if he did remember something, Hannah knew he'd lie so as not to be implicated. The objective with the initial questions was to unnerve him and see his genuine reaction when she accused him of sleeping with Casey.

"I heard she had a crush on you, as well as a few other students," Hannah said.

He stuttered, then stopped. "I've heard that throughout

the years, and it's very flattering, but I'm their teacher."

"Did you find her attractive?"

"I've been happily married to the love of my life for eighteen years, so I don't appreciate what you're implying."

If he was happily married, why wasn't he wearing a wedding ring? Why wasn't there a picture of his wife on his desk? Why was there no evidence of his marriage at all in the office?

Ignoring his last response, Hannah pressed on. "Do you have any theories about what happened to Casey?"

"No, I don't. I'm a scholar, not a police officer. And since I'm not an officer, I don't think I can help you anymore with your questions. And I also have a staff meeting in twenty minutes, so I'm going to have to ask you to leave."

"I understand, and I'd like to thank you for being so generous with your time. Could you answer just one more question for me?"

"Yes, fine," he said, not hiding his annoyance.

Leaning forward, Hannah gently rested her elbows on the desk. "Were you sleeping with Casey?"

Gregory shifted in the chair, and for the first time since Hannah had been in the office, he took his eyes off her. She could feel his contempt with her questioning, could feel the way he wanted to throw her out of the office.

"In all my years at this university, I've never heard of such an outlandish accusation."

"You didn't answer my question, Professor. Were you fucking my sister?" Hannah said, louder this time.

"Of course not! I never had an intimate relationship with Casey," he snapped.

"What about any other students? Have you ever slept with any of them?"

"I don't know who you think you are."

Hannah vaulted out of the chair and hovered over the

desk. "When I walked in, you were inches from slipping your hand down my pants, and you probably would've fucked me on this desk if I propositioned you, so I'm pretty sure you've fucked at least a student or two."

"You little bitch, get out of my office before I throw you out!"

Hannah was certain the professor was the kind of scumbag who used his position of authority to prey on young, impressionable female students, but her gut feeling was telling her that he was incapable of murder. And even with all of her mental disorders, she could always trust her gut. That never double-crossed her.

"I'm pretty sure you were fucking my sister, but I don't think you killed her. But if you did, I will find out, and I will make sure you spend the rest of your life in jail."

"Get out! Get the fuck out!"

On the drive back to the motel, Hannah was pulled over for what she assumed was speeding. There was no other reason she could think of, unless someone from the nursing home had seen her exiting the parking lot after stealing the scrubs and gotten a glimpse of her license plate.

The officer tapped on the driver's-side window, and as Hannah started to roll it down, he said, "What brings you to Wyoming?"

"May I ask why you pulled me over?" Hannah said, ignoring his question.

"Expired tags."

She cursed herself for not renewing the tags before she left Denver. It was a minor detail that should not have been forgotten, and something she'd obsess over now until she returned home.

"Again, what brings you to Wyoming?"

"Just visiting your lovely state," Hannah said artificially.

She watched as the officer examined the back seat. It seemed like he was searching for something specific.

"I already ran your plates and see that you're a private investigator from Denver," he said, turning back to her.

"That is true."

"Do you have a firearm in the vehicle?"

After a brief, dejected hesitation, Hannah said, "That is also true."

Taking a step back, the officer pronounced, "I'm going to ask you to slowly step out of the vehicle."

"Let me explain."

The officer took another step back and placed his hand on his pistol. "I'm not going to ask you again. Slowly open the door, then keep your hands where I can see them, and step out of the vehicle."

There was no talking her way out of the situation. She'd been pulled over with a concealed weapon, and even in a gun-friendly state like Wyoming, she could face jail time. She also didn't want to get shot. Rural redneck cops tended to be trigger-happy—fire first and ask questions later. People on routine traffic stops had gotten shot for a lot less. It was time to shut up, smile, and obey every order.

With great care, she opened the car door and stepped out, her palms chest height, facing the officer. Within seconds, he had Hannah against the hood and was frisking her.

"Where is the gun?" he yelled into her ear.

"It's in the fucking glovebox."

The officer grabbed her right hand and pulled it behind her, then handcuffed her wrist. Before she could react, he had her left wrist cuffed.

"Is this really fucking necessary?" Hannah said, louder now.

"Don't say another word." He shoved her toward the police cruiser.

About an hour later, she was sitting in an office inside the Albany County jail. The handcuffs were making her hands numb, and she could feel her pulse against the metal. Leaning back into the chair, she stared out the window, watching the clouds float by, cursing herself for not lying about the gun.

The door opened, and a man walked in. Hannah looked back and studied him. Her guess was that he was probably the sheriff, and by the looks of him, he wasn't from Wyoming. He resembled city folk more than a cowboy. Probably originally from Colorado, maybe California.

"Hello Hannah, I'm Sheriff Rick Harris. How are you doing today?"

Glaring up at him, she said, "Can you get these damn cuffs off before I lose a finger?"

"Yes, of course."

The sheriff unlocked the handcuffs, patted her on the back, then started walking to his desk. The indentations from the cuffs cut deep into her flesh. Hannah began rubbing her wrists to alleviate the pain and assist the blood flow.

He set the handcuffs on the desk so gently they didn't make a sound, then sat down directly across from Hannah.

"I have to apologize for Earl. He's, umm, a hell of an officer, but he does everything by the book."

"Oh, is that what you call a two-hundred-pound man manhandling a woman half his size, throwing her around like a ragdoll and treating her like a hardened criminal?"

"Again, I'm sorry for any treatment you deemed unnecessary. But you did have a concealed firearm in your vehicle, and that is a class two misdemeanor and can be punishable by up to twelve months in jail and a fine up to $1,000."

Hannah didn't respond.

"But the good news for you is that we're not going to press any charges."

"Gee, thanks."

Her wrists were still throbbing, and for a moment her mind began to wander.

"I've read about the outstanding detective work you did in Denver, and I'm pretty certain I know what you're doing up in this neck of the woods."

"Do enlighten me, Sheriff."

"Please call me Rick."

She shrugged. "Okay, Rick. Why do you think I'm here? And I'll give you a hint. It's sure as shit not for the weather."

"I'd guess you're trying to solve your sister's unsolved murder," he said, raising his eyebrows.

For a long while, too long maybe, Hannah pondered a response. He just waited, elbows on desk, fingers intertwined.

"In January," she said at last, "it will be ten years, and to my knowledge, there has never been a serious suspect. Not a single one. And your department is probably not any closer to solving it than the day it happened. And I'll bet the file hasn't been opened in years, and nearly everyone in this fucking hick town has forgotten about her. And I bet you wish it would disappear into thin air, but guess what? As long as I'm alive, it won't. And yes, the only reason I'm here is to solve Casey's murder, because if I don't, I guarantee that it'll never get solved."

"You know we're on the same side."

"Are you sure about that?"

The sheriff leaned far back in his chair and crossed his arms. "I am. I don't like having any unsolved murders in my county. And nothing would make me happier than that case being solved. Be it by you or one of my detectives. I'll give you anything you need—case files, access to any evidence—and you can talk to some of the old-timers who were on the force when it happened if you'd like."

"Were you sheriff back then?"

Hannah already knew the answer, but she wanted to see how he would respond.

"No, that was a little before my time. Sheriff Gary Wells would've been the one who was in charge during the initial investigation. He retired about five or six years ago. Last I heard, he was living on a small farm outside of Medicine Bow. Spends his summers fishing and winters hunting. Sounds like a nice little retirement if you ask me."

"Any chance I could get his number?"

"I personally don't have it, but let me go ask a couple of the fellas. I'm sure one of them has it. And if not, I probably can get it from someone down in HR."

The sheriff excused himself and left the office, closing the door behind him.

Through the window, Hannah watched as he spoke to three deputies at three different desks. At the third desk, Rick laughed, gave the deputy a rambunctious pat on the back, then disappeared out of view. Turning back, Hannah searched the office, finally ending on the desk. It was clean—the only items on it were a coffee mug with the Albany County police department logo and a keyboard, mouse, and monitor.

Leaning forward, Hannah reached across the desk and clicked a button on the mouse. The screen lit up—nothing but a login screen. The sheriff must've logged out before he left the room.

About ten minutes later, Rick walked back into the office. "He said he doesn't want to talk about anything over the phone, but if you want to drive up to his place, he'll talk to you in person. He'll be home for about the next three hours, so if you leave right now, you'll make it in plenty of time. Ever been to Medicine Bow? Got a map?"

"No, neither," she said, shaking her head.

Rick grabbed a pen and notepad and started drawing a map to the ex-sheriff's house. After he was finished, he showed the map to Hannah and repeated the directions, using the pen as a guide. Then he ripped out the piece of paper and handed it to her. Swiftly, she grabbed it and slipped it into her jean pocket.

"Oh, and one more thing before you go," he said.

"Yes?"

"Were you at Gables Nursing Home last night?"

"No, I sure wasn't. I was sitting on the bed in my motel room watching TV," she said with another shake of her head.

"That's strange. Because the girl who broke into the building and shoved a nurse to the ground in a resident's room has your same physical characteristics. And I'm pretty sure when I get a chance to review the video, it's going to be your pretty little face."

"Maybe it was my doppelganger," she said, shrugging.

The sheriff smirked. "That was a freebie, Hannah. So, for the rest of your time in Laramie, please don't do anything illegal, because next time, I will arrest you, and I really, really don't want to do that."

Hannah rose and took one step toward the door, then stopped. "Any chance I could get my gun back?"

"When hell freezes over," he said. Then he repeated it a little softer, while tapping on the desk.

As she drove along Highway 30 past towns like Bosler, Rock River, Wilcox, and Medicine Bow, Hannah saw businesses boarded up, dilapidated and decaying houses, and crumbling infrastructure. The demise of rural America. All dying towns that'd be full-on dead in the next ten or twenty years. Young adults would move away, searching for an economic future, and the old-timers would just slowly die off. Maybe someday the bison would reclaim the land that belonged to them hundreds of years ago.

At the only stoplight in Medicine Bow, someone in a truck with a "God Saves" sign spray-painted on a piece of plywood in the bed threw a McDonald's bag out the passenger window. Hannah chuckled—even Jesus freaks didn't give a fuck about the environment. The light turned green, and the truck left a cloud of black diesel smoke in the intersection.

Ten minutes north of Medicine Bow, Hannah turned off the highway and onto a dirt road. After driving over the bars of the cattle-guard, she stopped and rolled down the window. Silence. Nothing but her thoughts.

The land stretched for all the eye could see. There were no buildings, no trees or bodies of water—nothing green at all, for that matter. Just bitterbrush, cheatgrass, dirt, and an endless string of electric utility poles running across the horizon. It was where someone would live if they were attempting to escape civilization in hopes of never being found.

After three miles on the road, she came to a single-story house at the bottom of a valley in the middle of a vast, open countryside. For a long time, Hannah watched the house, and the land, and the sky. It was motionless, inert. It could've been a painting.

All of a sudden, an ugly feeling came over her. Only two people knew where she was going, the current sheriff and the ex-sheriff, and they both knew that she didn't have a firearm, and if they wanted her to stop asking questions about cold cases, this would be the place to do it. Thoughts started running through her head. Why didn't the sheriff arrest her, why was he so accommodating, why did she have to drive almost two hours to the middle of nowhere when the conversation could've been a phone call? She considered turning around, but she knew she wouldn't get another opportunity to speak to the man who was in charge of the investigation. After four long, deep breaths, she focused her eyes and continued along the dirt road.

About a hundred feet from the house, a dog jumped out from behind a dirt mound, dashed toward her car, and started growling. Startled, Hannah gasped and stopped the car. As the dog approached, it slowed to a walk and went silent. To her best guess it was an Australian Cattle Dog or large Border Collie.

She rolled down the window three inches, speaking in a soft voice. "Easy boy, easy boy. Everything is okay."

They stared at each other, and the dog didn't move or make a sound. After about twenty seconds, Hannah continued on the road, and the dog kept pace with the car until she parked in front of the house. Then it lay down about five feet from the driver's-side door.

The front door of the house opened, and a man appeared in the doorway for a second, then walked to the edge of the patio. He resembled Colonel Kurtz from *Apocalypse Now*. That worried her.

"You must be Hannah. Why don't you come on inside so we can talk?"

"What about him?" Hannah said, pointing at the dog.

"Oh, little Rex? No need to worry about him. His bark is worse than his bite."

Inside the house, it was dim and quiet. A picture frame sat on the desk behind Gary that held a family portrait: Gary, possibly accompanied by his wife and two kids—a boy and a girl—in front of a fifth wheel camper. Looking around, Hannah got the sense that a woman didn't live in the house. Maybe divorced, maybe dead.

They went into the kitchen, and he offered her something to drink, but Hannah declined. He poured himself a glass of tea, then sat down at the table. In the corner was a glass gun cabinet displaying six shotguns like prized trophies. He probably had a story about each gun, and how many animals he'd killed with it.

"Rick didn't give me a lot of details. He only said you were looking to ask some questions about the Casey Jacobs case."

Hannah looked into his eyes, searching for anything there, but they were dead, and she suspected they'd been that way for a long time.

"That's right. I'd like to know what you remember. And any possible theories or suspects that might've been left out of the case files. Hunches or anything that couldn't officially be documented."

Gary remained still for a long moment, then pulled a can of Copenhagen out of his front pocket and started packing it. "You know, the entire time I was sheriff, we never had a single female deputy or investigator. Not a one. Hell, I think the only ladies in the entire department were the 911 operators, but I guess times are changing." He jammed a mound of tobacco into his lower gum. "What's the interest in this one?"

"She was my sister."

"My deepest condolences to you and your family."

Hannah nodded.

"That was a tough one for the county, and for the state, and for myself. I was really hoping to solve that one before retirement, but it just wasn't in the cards," he continued. "I'll do my best with any questions, but to tell you the truth it's been at least five years since I set my eyes on anything relating to that homicide."

"Well, I'll stay away from the minutiae then."

Gary stared blankly and with his thumb and index finger twisted the edge of his mustache. It felt like he was staring through her. Hannah got the impression that she could sit at the table for an hour and ask fifty questions and probably not get a single meaningful answer.

She knew he didn't respect her. He probably didn't respect any woman. Probably considered women as second-class citizens who belonged in the kitchen. If he got drunk enough, he'd probably start preaching that the country would be a better place if women never had been given the opportunity to vote and how Roe vs. Wade should be overturned.

"Who did you consider the main suspect?" Hannah said.

"Unfortunately, we never had one."

Having read the case files more times than she could count, probably at least once a week for the last decade, Hannah was certain she knew the details better than anyone. They were details she wished she could erase from her memory.

The killer had entered through the patio door sometime after midnight, and was in the apartment from two to four hours. After he bound and gagged Casey, he vaginally raped her while wearing a condom, then either flushed it down the toilet or took it with him. Same with the wrapper. At some point he made a sandwich, then washed the dishes and placed them in the drying rack.

Then he went back into the bedroom and proceeded to stab Casey with a steak knife, leaving her for dead as he exited the apartment, never to be seen or heard again.

There wasn't a single piece of evidence. No fingerprints, no blood, no hair, no semen, and no footprints. And with it being in the late 1980s and Wyoming, no DNA samples were taken.

The responding officer didn't lock down the apartment, resulting in contamination of the crime scene. After Casey was discovered, at least a dozen police officers and first responders trampled throughout the apartment, on the patio, and in the courtyard and the snow surrounding the building. Not that a pristine crime scene would've changed the outcome, but it gave Hannah the impression that they were an incompetent small-town police force unprepared for a big-city murder.

Over the years, it'd received the cold case treatment—a new investigator searching for something new or something that was overlooked on occasion. Sometimes Hannah would even receive a phone call from whoever was working the case, but it always ended with the same result. Nothing.

"The initial investigation was nearly five months and didn't produce a single suspect? Bullshit. Come on, Sheriff, off the record, who do you think did it?"

After spitting into an empty soda can, Gary looked at her sideways. "Every fall, ten thousand kids arrive in Laramie, and almost 80 percent of them are from out of state. When the school year ends, they go home and then come back in the fall. And when they graduate, most of them leave and never come back. Rough math says about a thousand twenty-something males graduated three months after the murder, and a majority of them probably haven't ever stepped foot back in the state since. If I was a gambling man, that's where I'd put my money."

"On a University of Wyoming student?"

"One hundred percent."

"Did you ever investigate Professor Gregory Reynolds? I've heard allegations that he's slept with some of his students. Possibly Casey."

"Greg? No, he was never questioned or considered a suspect."

"But you've heard the allegations, right? I've been in town a few days and I'm already aware of them, so I'm guessing someone in your position of authority must've heard them through the grapevine at some point."

"Yes, I have heard them on occasion, and I can tell you that they're just a rumor. Nothing more."

"Are you sure about that?"

"Yes, I'm sure," he said sharply. "Gregory is a decorated and tenured professor, as well as someone I've known for almost twenty years, and someone I consider a friend." He spit then continued. "And even in the off chance the rumors are true, it's not illegal. Immoral, yes, but not illegal. He is a good man, and I'd do anything for him, and I guarantee he'd do the same for me."

Odd choice of words. "You're right, it's not illegal, but if he was having a sexual relationship with one of his students who was then murdered, shouldn't that at least be a reason to bring him in for questioning?"

"I wasn't going to smear the man's reputation. No one has ever filed a complaint with the school, and he doesn't have as much as a speeding ticket, let alone a police report for anything nefarious. I'd put my career and reputation that he is completely innocent and had nothing to do with Casey's murder."

They stared at each other for a while before she spoke again.

"So, your working theory is that some college kid murdered Casey and packed up and left town after graduation. And now the case is unsolvable? How convenient for you and your department."

He spit again. "You think I'm some incompetent hick cop, don't you?"

"No, no I don't," she said with an even voice.

That was a lie. It was nothing against the man, but she thought most law enforcement officers were incompetent. Immoral, power-hungry, and lazy were a few other terms that came to mind.

"While I was sheriff, 99 percent of the murder cases that happened in Albany County were solved. That is the highest percentage in the history of the county for a sheriff, and the third highest in the history of the state. The only two I didn't solve was Casey's and a prostitute who was chopped into pieces and put into a dumpster behind a truck stop on the outskirts of town. And the only reason I didn't solve either of those was because I'm certain the perpetrator doesn't reside in Wyoming."

Hannah was about to respond, but Gary raised his hand and cut her off.

"Now you listen to me. You can call me a lot of things, but incompetent is not one of them." His voice grew louder as he spoke.

Nervously, Hannah nodded, then cleared her throat and said, "Did you ever question Dorothy Bennett?"

"We questioned over a hundred people, and I don't remember every single name of the hundred. So, I'm not sure if we did or not."

"You didn't, and she lived directly above Casey, and she saw a suspicious man at the complex around the time of the murder and she never saw him again. White, in his thirties with a long beard. And as she watched him, he sped out of the parking lot in a black or blue Ford F-150."

"A middle-aged white male with a beard, driving an F-150? That's the description of about half the men who live in Wyoming," he said, chuckling. "That and fifty cents will get you a Coke."

"It was a lead you didn't follow up on."

"I can't tell you why we didn't talk to her, but I am sure there was a very good reason. I do know there were over fifty leads we fully investigated and they were nothing but dead ends. And to answer your question, I don't think it's unsolvable, but it's going to be from someone getting drunk and running their mouth or someone who knows about the murder and the guilt becomes too much to live with and they call in and confess, or some deathbed confession." He paused. "And in my opinion, without some random dumb luck, it'll remain a cold case forever."

"I think you're wrong. It will be solved, and when I do, it's going to look really bad on you and your former department."

He smiled. "I think you should get going. It's going to be dark soon, and I do not advise driving these dirt roads at night—they can be very dangerous. So, unless you have any other pressing questions, I'd suggest you be on your way."

About twenty miles south of River Rock, on a long, deserted two-lane stretch of Highway 30, headlights appeared in the rearview mirror, off in the long distance. The occasional oncoming traffic would drive by, but Hannah hadn't seen a single car in the southbound lane since she turned onto the highway thirty miles ago.

At first, she ignored the lights, but within minutes, the vehicle had erased the distance. It was barreling in at a high rate of speed—five car lengths, four, three, then finally two.

It looked like the brights were on, and the closer the vehicle got, the more it blinded Hannah. She flipped the night mode switch on the rearview mirror and got a glimpse of the vehicle. It was a dark, full-sized truck. Her whole body went tense. Maybe it was the truck she was looking for, or maybe it was nothing but a hostile driver, or maybe it was Sheriff Wells coming to run her off the road.

Fixated on the mirror, she watched as the truck played a game of cat and mouse. Coming within a car length, then dropping back to a hundred feet, then returning at high speed and starting to cross the double line like it was going to pass her, only to fall back behind her car again. This behavior went on for miles. At one point, Hannah thought the truck was going to strike her bumper and hurl her into the ditch.

Reaching across the center console, Hannah opened the glovebox and removed a pair of brass knuckles and rested them on her thigh.

"Come on, fucker," she said, her jaw clenched, looking into the mirror.

Glancing back at the road, she saw a deer standing like a statue—half on the road, half on the shoulder. Hannah jerked the steering wheel, pulling the car into the middle of the road, narrowly avoiding the animal and nearly losing control. The truck followed like a shadow.

Moments later, the truck crossed the double yellow lines and started to pass Hannah. She gripped the steering wheel with both hands, preparing for an impending collision.

When the truck passed, Hannah looked into the cab at the middle-aged woman who was driving and smoking a cigarette. They made brief eye contact, and the woman shook her head in disapproval. Peering down to the needle on the speedometer, Hannah saw it was hovering at fifty-nine, four above the speed limit. She extended her middle finger and leaned back into the headrest.

Within minutes, the taillights vanished into the night, and Hannah was driving on the highway alone.

As she approached Laramie, the city illuminated the horizon, a haze of light pollution surrounded by a vast, great black emptiness.

On the outskirts of town, Hannah stopped at the first liquor store she found. Inside, she grabbed a bottle of Jack Daniel's and a two-liter of Coke. Up until recently, she'd despised the taste of whiskey, but it'd grown on her, becoming her drink of choice. Probably because sipping on it reminded her of Marshall.

The clerk, a man in his early twenties, decent looking, started flirting with her. Complimenting her hair, asking what she was doing in Laramie and if she needed any restaurant or bar recommendations. She just stared blankly back. In one ear, out the other. Being able to utterly ignore, then politely end conversations was one of her talents as an introvert.

"Thanks for the suggestions," she said, grabbing the bag.

It was a short drive from the liquor store to the motel, and after dropping off her backpack, she grabbed the ice bucket and walked to the vending machine room. Next to the ice machine was the visitor guides display rack with brochures of four-wheeling, rafting, fly-fishing, and various other outdoor activities. For a moment, she doubted herself and her ability to solve the case, and contemplated skipping town and going on one of the brochure adventures. Then she turned back and pressed the ice machine button.

Back in the room, she grabbed a plastic cup, dropped in a handful of ice, and filled the cup with whiskey until it was almost overflowing. Sitting on the edge of the bed, she took a long swallow, then another. Then another.

An hour later, she had slammed three stiff drinks and was in a cycle of endless channel surfing. Finally, she stopped on an episode of *The Real World* on MTV. She watched the last ten minutes before turning off the TV and tossing the remote to the foot of the bed.

She stood up clumsily and pulled off her belt, then slid out of her pants and crashed back down on the mattress. She looked in the cup for a second, then chugged the rest of the whiskey and tossed it across the room. The partially melted ice cubes bounced across the carpet like a pair of dice.

Lying on the bed, she closed her eyes and started running her fingers across her scars, romanticizing about each cut. Some cuts were because she'd been alone, and some cuts were because she'd been scared, and some cuts were because she'd been depressed, but a lot of the cuts were because she'd wanted to feel alive. Cutting was her Prozac—a way to feel normal, relatively speaking.

It'd been something like eight months since a blade touched her skin. Eight fucking months. Long enough to switch from days to months. That accomplishment deserved a medal.

Never had she gone that long, and after the Megan Floyd case, the urge had diminished, and she thought that phase of her life was over, but eventually it returned, as strong as ever. Back with her day and night.

She wondered if the thoughts would ever stop. She couldn't imagine having the urge when she was a senior citizen, but maybe she would—well, if she lived that long.

She knew if she didn't pass out, the obsession would

become unmanageable, and she'd scour the room for something sharp enough to cut her skin. And she didn't want that to happen.

"Not tonight," she slurred.

Not tonight, hopefully not ever again.

Hannah grabbed the top pillow and slid it between her legs, squeezing it like she was wrapping her legs around another person. Then she slipped on her headphones and pressed play on the Discman. As she closed her eyes, the opening chords of "Nutshell" by Alice in Chains began.

THREE

The sun was peering through the blinds onto the brown carpet. Hannah glared at the sunspot on the floor, her head pounding, heart racing, mouth parched. On the nightstand stood the half-empty bottle of whiskey. She stared at it for a bit and considered pouring the rest of the alcohol down the bathroom sink. After a minute or two, she rolled over and began rubbing her eyes, a poor attempt to alleviate the headache. The only remedies, of course, were aspirin and sleep.

Two loud knocks sounded on the door. Hannah sprang off the bed and started searching the room for her gun, only to remember that it was somewhere in the Albany County police station evidence hold. As she tip-toed across the carpet, she heard two more pounding knocks.

"It's housekeeping," a woman said with a heavy Spanish accent.

Hannah opened the door and smiled. "No service today, thank you."

"Mañana?"

"Yes, mañana," Hannah said.

As she was closing the door, Hannah stopped and said, "Would you happen to have any aspirin? Aspirina?"

She stared for a moment, then nodded. "Sí."

The maid grabbed an aspirin packet off the housekeeping cart and handed it over. Hannah thanked her, then went into the bathroom, tore open the packet, turned on the faucet, filled a plastic cup, and swallowed the tablets.

Hannah staggered back into the room and sat at the edge of the bed. Her head pounded with every beat. After a long exhale, she buried her face into the pillow. The day could wait. She decided to sleep for another hour, maybe two. Then, hopefully, the hangover would subside and she'd be able to resume the investigation.

Sometime around noon, Hannah rolled out of bed and made her way to the shower. With water cascading down her face, she closed her eyes and allowed her thoughts to be consumed by the case. As much as she hated to admit it, Gary was right about one thing—the case was as cold as they came, and it'd take nothing short of a miracle to solve it. She had exactly one clue after talking to about a dozen people and driving halfway across the state.

"A man in the truck," she said, frustration slipping through her lips.

After getting dressed and doing her makeup, Hannah sat on the bed and started flipping channels again, stopping on *Wheel of Fortune*. She attempted the puzzles but was stumped with each one. Spelling wasn't a strong suit.

It was only the third day, yet doubt had already begun to creep into her mind. Did she really think she could solve this case when so many before her had failed? Instead of immersing herself in the investigation, she found herself succumbing to mindless procrastination, aimlessly watching daytime television.

Somewhere, the persistent hum of a vacuum cleaner penetrated through the walls. The monotonous drone of the motor put her in a tranquil state, the high decibels assisting in drowning out the thoughts in her head.

When the noise ceased, she decided to grab lunch before starting the day's investigation. She wasn't hungry, but knew she needed something in her stomach. After briefly weighing her options, she decided to walk to the grocery store for a sandwich and a bag of chips.

On the walk, the wind howled against Hannah's face, seemingly stronger with each passing minute. She cursed herself for not driving and thought about turning back, but walking was her meditation—it allowed her to think.

Maybe it was the wind, or maybe it was her anxiety, but ten blocks from the motel she sensed that she was being followed. She stopped and looked into the window of a gift shop. Handbags, jewelry, candles and some Christmas ornaments and stockings. After a moment, she glanced back to the sidewalk, and the only person was a woman pushing a stroller. Hannah watched her for a second, then turned back to the store.

She pretended to search for something in her purse, and as the woman walked past, Hannah nodded. She watched the woman turn the corner and disappear out of view. There was something about the town that made Hannah feel uneasy, paranoid. Small towns made her feel trapped; she required skyscrapers and a steady stream of rush-hour traffic.

For a long time, she watched the street and saw nothing. Then she darted between two cars, crossed the street, and continued to the grocery store, carefully watching the cracks in the pavement.

On her way back to the motel, Hannah again felt that she was being followed. This time, she continued walking until the end of the block, then turned a corner, placed the brown grocery bag on the ground, and flattened herself against the wall. She listened carefully, and about twenty seconds later, a man turned the corner and looked directly at her. For a second, he froze. Then he looked like he was about to speak, but he only smiled and awkwardly stepped away from Hannah, hurrying down the sidewalk. Hannah grabbed the bag and started after the man.

"Why the fuck are you following me?" she called, her voice rough.

"I wanted to get a better look at you," the man said, not looking back.

"And why is that?"

"I wanted to see if you were Hannah Jacobs."

Hannah clenched the man's biceps, half turning him. "Who the fuck are you?"

Squeezing hard, she dug her fingernails into his skin. He let out a tiny whimper.

"My name's Tony Singleton," he rushed to say, staring at her hand around his arm.

"Okay, Tony. That was part one, now answer part two. Why are you following me? And if I don't believe you, I'll knee you in the balls so hard you won't feel them for a month."

There was perhaps a second of silence, and then he said, "You're Hannah Jacobs, right? So umm, I wanted to talk to you about your sister's murder."

She studied him for a moment. "Oh really? What would you like to discuss?"

"I think I might have a suspect."

Hannah released her grip and took a step back. "Who?"

Tony scanned the street, looking for anyone who

might be eavesdropping. His voice grew hushed. "Can we go somewhere to talk?"

They sat at a table in the rear of Coal Creek Café, each with a cup of drip coffee in front of them. With a spoon, Hannah gradually stirred the coffee about ten times, then picked up her cup, blew into it for a moment, and took a sip.

From a table over her shoulder, Hannah overheard a couple discussing their financial issues. Behind on rent, credit cards maxed out, utilities about to be turned off. Hannah didn't want to eavesdrop, but her obsessive-compulsive disorder made it almost impossible not to. For as long as she could remember, she'd heard everything within earshot—no conversations could be filtered out.

"How did you know who I was?" Hannah said.

"I'm a cook at Annie's Diner, and Nancy told me that she had a conversation with you. And since this town is pretty much nothing more than a college campus, a couple gas stations, and a dozen motels, it wasn't that difficult to find you."

Hannah stared at him. There were too many people who knew her name, and why she was in town, and probably the car she drove, and most likely the motel she was staying at. And if they knew the motel, they could easily obtain the room number. She considered switching motels but decided that it wouldn't make a difference. If someone really wanted to find her, it'd wouldn't be that difficult in Laramie.

"And you just decided to follow me? Then what?"

"I really didn't have a plan. I just wanted to get a closer look to make sure it was you, and when I was sure it was, I was going to ask if you wanted to talk. And here we are."

Tony took a drag off a cigarette and exhaled. A cloud of smoke hung in the air, dividing them.

"Why'd you try to run when I confronted you on the street?"

"I don't know—instincts, I guess," he said with a nervous bark of laughter.

Hannah watched the man closely, unsure if he was there with good intentions or something more heinous.

"I really don't have time for games, so let's see what you got."

"Fine," he said, clearing his throat. "Have you ever heard of the High Plain Murders?"

"No," Hannah said, shaking her head.

"Not surprising, most people haven't. It's the name me and my fellow amateur sleuths came up with for a series of murders that have occurred in this region over the last decade."

"Amateur sleuths? Or maybe crackpots who live in their parents' basement and obsess about unsolved murders," Hannah said sharply.

"Call us whatever you want, but I think we've uncovered something the cops, and the FBI, and whoever else has worked these murders, has missed," he said, shrugging.

He had been speaking slowly the whole time, as if on a three-quarter-speed setting. Hannah suspected he was a pothead or had suffered some sort of brain damage.

Tony unzipped a shoulder bag and pulsed out a three-ring binder. After licking his fingers, he opened the binder and flipped to the fourth page. Hannah watched intently.

"Alice Sanders in '91, Denise Long and Judy Meyers in '94, Diana Allen in '96, Julia Boone last May, and Casey was the first in 1989."

"You're telling me there is a serial killer in Wyoming that only you and your buddies know about?"

A serial killer was a theory that Hannah had never considered. She always assumed Casey knew the killer.

An infatuated co-ed, or a professor, or a co-worker, or a customer, or someone who lived in her apartment complex. But what always perplexed Hannah was the glaring absence of evidence and witnesses. Because if it were the work of a one-off, first-time killer, odds were they would have slipped up somewhere, leaving behind something that would've led to their arrest.

"I'm telling you there are six unsolved murders over the last ten years—four in Wyoming, one in South Dakota, and one in Colorado," Tony said.

"And what makes you think all these murders are related to each other?"

"All female. All under thirty. All of them were Caucasian and short-haired brunettes, and very attractive. All of them were single and living alone. All but one of the murders happened at night and in the victim's apartment. All were raped and either stabbed or strangled. All of them missing a piece of jewelry, a necklace or earrings. And do you know your astronomy?"

"A little," Hannah said.

"Well, all of the murders happened on a waning crescent moon."

"Doesn't that happen like once a month?"

"Yes, approximately every twenty-six days. And if that was the only thing that connected the murders, I'd be the first one to say it was a random coincidence, but there are all those other details that connect the girls. Here, let me show you a few things."

He flipped to the middle of the binder and removed a regional map, then unfolded it. Each murder had a piece of masking tape with the name and age of each victim, along with the date and method of the homicide. Using a pen as a pointer, he started circling locations while saying the victim's name. Laramie, Gillette, Rapid City, South

Dakota, Cheyenne, Greeley, Colorado, and Medicine Bow National Forest, an hour west of Laramie.

Hannah made mental notes of each victim.

"A girl was abducted from a National Forest? If there is a serial killer, this one doesn't seem like it's connected to the others," Hannah said.

"Yeah, I went back and forth on that one, but everything else fits. Young, attractive, short brown hair—looked almost identical to the third victim, Denise Long. She lived alone in an apartment about a mile from here. And she was raped and strangled to death on a waning crescent moon."

Flipping through three more pages, he stopped at photocopies of newspaper clippings detailing each murder. The story for Casey had a small black-and-white photo of her underneath the headline. Tony looked at the picture, then looked at Hannah.

"Jesus, I didn't realize until just now, but you look exactly like Casey," Tony said.

Hannah started to blush. She'd always considered her sister beautiful. Growing up, she yearned to possess just a fraction of that beauty.

"Thanks," she murmured, looking away.

"And don't try to tell me all these girls don't look like they're related. Hell, they could've been sisters, or at least cousins."

Hannah studied the pictures for a long while, chills running down her spine. Tony was right—they all had a striking resemblance to each other.

"Can I see this?" she asked, reaching for the binder, not waiting for a response.

"Umm, sure?"

Hannah started skimming, scanning each page before flipping to the next one. Some of the pages were official internal Albany County documents.

"How did you get these?"

"Let's just say I have a friend down at the courthouse," Tony said with a smirk.

"Tell me about the last girl," Hannah said, still skimming.

"Julia Boone."

"Yes, Julia Boone," Hannah repeated softly, making another mental note.

From across the table, Tony turned to the pages pertaining to Julia.

Julia Marie Boone, age twenty-six, born March 18, 1973 in Pueblo, Colorado at Saint Mary-Corwin Hospital. A graduate at the University of Wyoming in 1995 with a degree in accounting who worked part-time at Wyoming Bank & Trust and nights as a bartender at Buffalo Saloon, both in downtown Laramie. She was an avid long-distance runner who completed numerous marathons throughout the region. Julia was an only child, whose parents had divorced when she was seven. Her father died in a single car accident a month after she was murdered, his blood alcohol content three times the legal limit. As for her mother, her whereabouts remained unknown.

On the day of her disappearance, Julia had traveled to Medicine Bow National Forest to do an eight-mile out-and-back hike. She left her apartment sometime after two in the afternoon and was never seen again. Her car was found in the trailhead parking lot untouched, and her body was discovered the next morning on a park bench in LaBonte Park in Laramie.

"The park located in the middle of town?" Hannah said.

"The very one."

"So, he follows the girl into the forest, abducts her, rapes and kills her, then dumps her body in a very public location." Hannah took a moment. "Why did he change his MO with this girl?" she said, thinking aloud.

Just then, Hannah felt like someone was watching them from the parking lot, but when she turned, it was virtually empty.

Tony shrugged. "I don't have the slightest idea."

If it was a serial killer who'd murdered Casey, Hannah knew it'd be easier to solve the most recent murder. Julia's murder was still an active homicide investigation, while Casey's file was in a box in a police department basement collecting dust, long ago forgotten by almost everyone.

"She was a local. Did you know her?"

"Not directly, but I know someone who is friends with her best friend."

"What's the best friend's name?"

"Stacy Holt. Last I heard, she quit her job and moved up to somewhere in Montana."

"Would you happen to have a phone number for her?"

"Sweetie, I enjoy doing the research, but I'm not about to contact a victim's friend or family."

"And the two girls in '94, was there any connection between them?"

"Not that I found. The distance between the murders was the farthest of any two, almost four hundred miles. They both grew up and lived in the town where they were murdered, and there was no connection between family, friends, job, or anything else. I highly doubt they ever met each other."

"Were there any reports of anyone seeing a black or blue Ford F-150 before or during any of the murders?"

Tony tapped his nose for a moment. "Not that I remember. Why?"

"Just a lead that's probably nothing. Do you have any suspects in that report?"

Tony shook his head. "Unfortunately, that's where my investigation skills shit the bed."

Hannah glanced at the window and could see her reflection. Her face looked thin. Thinner than she remembered.

"How many people know about this serial killer theory you've came up with?" she asked.

Tony glanced up at the ceiling and started doing the math in his head. "Five, probably eight at the most. But I'd say I've spent more time investigating this case than all the other guys combined."

"And have you gone to the police about your theory?"

"I've tried numerous times, but they don't want to listen to a guy like me."

"And why is that?"

"Because I'm black, and I'm a stoner, and I'm gay. Sweetie, that's three strikes in Wyoming. I'm lucky they haven't tossed me in jail and thrown away the key," he said, taking a drag. "Look what happened to Matthew. If it wasn't for the media attention, they probably would've given those guys a slap on the wrist. Probably manslaughter or some bullshit like that."

"Those fuckers should've gotten the death penalty," Hannah said.

Tony nodded. "You have to remember Hannah, for people like me, Wyoming is worlds apart from Denver. Living here is like being stuck in a time machine that's set to the '80s."

Hannah sat silent for a second, tapping her coffee cup, unsure how to respond. "I take it you're not from here."

"Nah, Chicago. I moved here five years ago for school but dropped out after the first semester. Something about waking up early and going to class doesn't work for me."

"Please don't take this the wrong way, but if you're not

going to school and your family is back in Chicago, what keeps you here?"

"I hate big city life and love me some cowboys."

Hannah laughed. She liked Tony, but more importantly, she felt like she could trust him.

"What do you think of Sheriff Harris?" Hannah said.

"How can I say this nicely? He's an asshole who's more interested in busting people for smoking weed and getting drunk than real crimes like murders and kidnappings. Quantity over quality, you know? You should try your best to keep your distance from him and his goons."

"Thanks for the advice."

"That's what I'm here for."

"Do you think I could borrow this for a day or two?" she said, tapping on the binder.

"No, but I'll let you copy whatever you want—as long as you're paying for it."

"Deal."

About thirty minutes and five dollars in dimes later, Hannah stood on the sidewalk in front of the Albany County Public Library, holding a stack of warm, freshly printed copies of every page from Tony's report.

"Hopefully there's some gold in here," Hannah said.

"You bet your ass there is. And if it helps you find the killer, you owe me dinner."

Hannah smiled. "If it does, I'll take you to Hawaii."

"Let me see that real quick," Tony said, pointing at the copies.

She handed them to him, and he removed a pen from behind his ear.

"Here's my number and address. My apartment is literally five blocks from here. Don't hesitate to call or stop by if you have any questions or if you want a second set of eyes to look at something. Now I gotta get running or else I'm going to be late for work. Be safe out there, Hannah."

"I will."

Tony was about five steps away when Hannah called his name. "Oh, one more question. Do you know anywhere I could get a gun?" she said in a hushed tone, making a gun figure with her hand.

"Honey, I'm a lover, not a fighter," he said.

Back at the motel, Hannah neatly stacked the copies and placed them on the floor next to the bed. Then she grabbed her notebook, a pen, and a pink highlighter, as well as the bottle of whiskey and a plastic cup, and slid onto the floor, sitting cross-legged in front of the stack. Leaning against the bed, she licked her fingers and picked up the top copy. She read each page at least twice, some of them three or four times.

After reading the last page, Hannah placed it on the stack and leaned back, trying to comprehend everything she'd read. Every word, every girl, every murder. Every single murder. Motionless, she sat for a long while, long enough to completely lose track of time. Her legs were asleep, numb to the world. As she massaged her thighs, she gazed down onto the top page, her eyes going in and out of focus on the vibrant streaks of the highlighter.

When she'd arrived in town, she thought she'd be chasing a ghost. Coming to Laramie was more for her mental health than anything, because she knew that deep down, she couldn't live with herself if she didn't make an effort to investigate the case in the very town where it had happened.

Her expectations were modest. At most, she'd get a

lead or two, maybe someone who'd overheard a story, or secondhand gossip. Maybe if she was lucky, she'd talk to someone who knew someone who knew someone who thought they knew who the killer was, but eventually all those leads would die just like the Colorado summer wildflowers, and she'd go home to Denver and attempt to close this unsettling chapter of her life.

But after reading Tony's files, she felt closer than ever to finding Casey's murderer. There was a monster somewhere in Wyoming, and she was determined to find him. And for the first time since arriving in Laramie, a newfound sense of hope washed over her. A hope that she might solve the murder.

Glancing at the copies on the floor, Hannah fixated on a few pages that jutted out from the stack. She picked up the stack and methodically sorted and shuffled it against her knees. After she was content, she placed the perfectly arranged stack on the floor.

"Come on Hannah, you can't stop now. You're starting to get close to this fucker," she said.

Reaching to the floor, she grabbed her notebook and started flipping through the notes she'd made. Six murders spanning over ten years, in three states and five counties. And if the murders were done by a single serial killer, there were probably more, and there would be more to come. Probably until the killer was caught, killed or died.

None of these victims were random—they were selected carefully, with precision, and in his fucked-up mind probably a degree of love. They were all connected in some way, probably only known to the killer.

At first, Hannah considered the likelihood that it was a drifter, someone who used the train or bus networks to jump from town to town. Or maybe a drug addict who slipped in and out of psychosis. Meth was prevalent in this part of the country.

"No, no," she whispered.

If it was a drifter or drug addict, the murders would've been random, and messy, and the perpetrator would've slipped up and left a clue at one of the crime scenes—a fingerprint, traces of semen, fingernail or hair or blood samples, something that would've led to an eventual identification.

It was someone who had patience to select the perfect victims, and someone in control of the urge. Waiting until what he deemed was the ideal time, and when they were alone and most vulnerable, he'd strike. The murders were not impulsive; they took time. Weeks, months, or maybe years.

He would've been observing their routines, meticulously following their every move. From their workplaces or schools to the grocery stores, the post office and restaurants they frequented, blending into the background. Perhaps he even engaged in casual interactions with each victim, offering a courteous greeting and small talk.

If Casey was his first, he must've rehearsed that night over and over again in his head, leaving nothing to chance. That type of planning meant he was intelligent, with an above-average IQ. It also meant he was at least thirty or forty, maybe older. The sophistication of the crimes was not something a young adult could pull off. Most likely single or in a loveless relationship. Definitely white, because serial killers were almost always white males, not to mention the population of Wyoming was 92 percent Caucasian.

The first five victims were killed in their apartments. They were always alone, each living in a first-floor or garden-level apartment that he accessed from a patio door or living room screen window. For each murder, he remained in the apartment for two to four hours. Each victim was raped, always with a condom. Sometimes he ate a sandwich or a snack, sometimes showered. The times he showered, he took the towel with him. He always cleaned the dishes and always took the condom and condom wrapper.

Besides the body and the missing deli meat, the killer didn't leave a trace. He was aware of DNA—maybe an ex-cop or someone who studied forensic science. He probably knew that small-town police departments were naive, lacking the expertise to solve complex murders, and that it'd be near impossible for them to connect murders that were across state lines and outside their jurisdictions.

Maybe not a wealthy person, but probably someone who was financially stable enough to stalk each victim until he deemed it was the perfect moment to strike.

Possibly an oil field worker, or a truck driver like Robert Ben Rhoades, The Truck Stop Killer, who was convicted of four murders, and possibly committed as many as fifty. All of the murders had occurred in cities that were adjacent to or near an interstate.

She tapped on the notebook with her pen.

Then the Great Basin Killer came to mind. All the victims were around the same age, sexually assaulted and then murdered by strangulation or stabbing, but that was where the similarities ended. The key difference was the disposal of the victims. All were found in desolate locations like deserts and rivers, far away from civilization.

The room was hot and humid, and beads of sweat were dripping down her forehead. Hannah grabbed the sleeve of her shirt and wiped her eyes. Glancing at the thermostat, she contemplated turning down the heat but decided against it, knowing she'd wake up in the middle of the night, freezing.

Laying the pictures of victims two to six side by side, Hannah stared at them for a long time, running her index finger in a circular motion on the carpet below them. All the girls had striking similarities in their appearance: eye color, hair color, hair length. Even their smiles were nearly identical.

Hannah picked up the pictures of Julia and of Alice, the second victim, and stared at them side by side, shifting her eyes back and forth between the two. After twenty seconds, she laid Alice's picture facedown, then picked up the picture of Denise, the third victim. After staring at those two side by side, she laid the picture of Denise facedown and did a side by side of Julia with the final two victims. All of the girls were pretty, but not pretty enough to make the national news circuit of Larry King and Nancy Grace. That took a special type of beauty.

Flipping through the folder, Hannah stopped on the section pertaining to Julia, rereading the pages for the third time.

Less than seven months separated Hannah's and Julia's birthdays. They both should've been entering the prime years of their lives. But Julia was dead, and Hannah was fighting off her demons every day to stay alive.

A little after ten o'clock on the morning of her disappearance, Julia had called her best friend Stacy Holt to confirm dinner plans that evening and inform her that she was going to do a hike at Medicine Bow National Forest, about an hour east of her apartment in Laramie. That was the last known contact with her.

When she didn't arrive for dinner, Stacy drove to her apartment. Not seeing her friend's car, she called 911. Dispatch contacted an off-duty deputy who lived about ten miles from the trailhead, and within thirty minutes, her car was located. That was around eight thirty, and by best estimate, she'd only been missing for four or five hours.

The initial working theory was that she'd gotten lost or succumbed to an injury on the trail. At that elevation, and time of year, night temperatures dropped to the low twenties, so it was crucial to commence a preliminary search effort. The deputy, along with a neighbor, searched eight miles of the trail with flashlights and headlamps, yelling her name until their throats became hoarse. Sometime after midnight, they decided to suspend the search effort until the following morning.

As search and rescue was mobilizing a search party of approximately forty individuals, a trashman driving past LaBonte Park a little after six that morning saw what he at first thought was a mannequin. Instead, it was Julia's lifeless, naked body, draped there on a park bench. The search party was immediately called off, and the homicide investigation began. This was all less than twelve hours after the 911 call and around twenty hours after Julia called Stacy about her hiking agenda. And just like Casey's homicide nearly a decade earlier, there was no suspect, and virtually zero clues.

"Why did you decide to leave her on display in a public location?" she whispered.

Hannah stretched to the nightstand and opened the bottom drawer. Then she pulled out the White Pages and flipped to the start of the H's. After flipping two more pages, she ran her finger down the page, finally stopping on "Holt." There were only two listings. She wrote each address and phone number into her notebook, then wrote "Stacy" followed by three question marks.

Hannah finished her drink in two gulps, then pushed off the floor and rose to her feet. As she stood, the blood rushed to her head and she became lightheaded. She hadn't realized how drunk she'd gotten. Probably at least four drinks. Maybe five. Slowly, she sat back down, the room slightly spinning.

After some time, she went to the window, then pushed aside the curtain a couple of inches. Ten cars were spread across the parking lot, and not another person in sight. The absence of activity gave her an unnerving feeling. In the far corner of the lot, a streetlight flickered, like something out of an Alfred Hitchcock movie. It was mesmerizing, and Hannah watched it for longer than she'd have liked to admit.

Glancing down at her watch, she saw that it was a little after nine. To her best recollection, the last time she'd had anything to eat was lunch, nearly nine hours ago. Forgetting to eat seemed to be happening more and more.

Hannah grabbed her purse and slipped the room key into her pocket. Stepping out, she eased the door shut behind her. But after taking one step, a wave of panic washed over her. She jolted back, reached for the doorknob, and turned it three times.

For the last year, she hadn't been able to leave her apartment, or car, or a motel room without triple checking that the door was locked. And the obsessive-compulsive tendencies seemed to be getting worse—checking the door multiple times, washing her hands dozens of times throughout the day, sometimes for minutes.

She had read stories of people cleaning their apartment for hours or washing their hands until they nearly bled, or people who couldn't step foot outside, prisoners in their own home. The mere thought of her own tendencies escalating to that level haunted her, keeping her awake many nights.

After checking the doorknob one final time, Hannah looked up and saw a man, probably close to her age, leaning against the railing and smoking a cigarette. He was three doors down, in front of room 221. The man was tall, slender, and very attractive, with a touch of danger. Brad Pitt had nothing on him. He glanced at her for a second, then brought the cigarette to his lips and took a drag without blinking. Hannah half waved and began to turn away.

"How are you doing tonight?" the man said, ashing the cigarette over the railing.

Their eyes met as she swung her head back, and then Hannah averted her gaze to the walkway. Maintaining eye contact for more than a couple of seconds with strangers often triggered her anxiety. Sometimes she felt uncomfortable in her own skin. This was one of those times.

"What was that?" she said.

She'd heard him, but that was a response she'd give when she was unsure how to answer someone's question. It was her way of buying a few extra moments to formulate an intelligent reply.

The man pushed off the railing and stepped toward her. "I just asked how your night is going."

"Oh, it's fine, just doing some reading, and about to grab something to eat. You?"

"Just drinking some beers and pondering how I ended up in Wyoming." He took a quick drag. "What are you reading?"

She scratched her neck, then spoke gingerly. "It's a research paper for work."

"Work huh? How's that going?"

"So far, so good."

"What type of work do you do?"

"Umm, I'd rather not say," she said. She wasn't sure why she didn't want to tell him.

"Fair enough," he said. A long exhale followed. "Could I at least get your name in case we run into each other again?"

"It's Hannah."

Neither of them said a word. The only sound was the buzz of the streetlights and the drone of semi-truck engines on the highway.

Finally, he said, "I'm Mark, by the way, if you were wondering."

Hannah smiled, hesitant, unsure how to respond. She was always awkward when first meeting attractive members of the opposite sex, never knowing what to say or how to act. Cupping her mouth, she cleared her throat. Another nervous trait.

Just as Hannah was about to tell him what she was doing in Laramie, the man said, "Well, I don't want to keep you from your work, so have a good night."

"You do the same," Hannah said nodding.

The man leaned back against the railing. Hannah stood frozen for a second, then turned with a touch of awkwardness and began making her way toward the stairs. As she turned the corner, she threw a glance over her shoulder at the man, keeping her eyes on him until he was out of sight.

After grabbing a bag of BBQ chips, a Snickers bar and two Cokes, she returned to the walkway but Mark was gone. Disappointment washed over her, and she briefly considered knocking on his door. She longed for the simple pleasure of casual interaction and the playful banter of flirting with someone. But she felt unattractive, and after days without putting on makeup or even brushing her hair, confidence was lacking at the moment. Nonetheless, she made a promise to herself that if she ran into him again, she'd invite him to get a drink.

In the room, Hannah poured about half a can of Coke into the plastic cup, then topped it off with the rest of the whiskey bottle. She nestled the bottle into the trash can before sitting down on the edge of the bed to sip on the drink. Tearing open the candy bar, she took three bites, then placed the remainder on the nightstand.

Hannah reached for the phone and dialed Tony's number. As it rang, she started tapping in rhythm on her knee with her thumb. After the fifth ring, the answering machine picked up.

"This is Tony, but unfortunately for you I'm not home. Please leave your name and number and maybe I'll call you back. Maybe."

There was a beep, and Hannah was about to speak, but she stopped. It was late, and she was drunk, and overzealous, nearing what some would consider manic. No need to sound like a deranged person on an answering machine. She'd call tomorrow when she was sober.

Between her legs, she spun the pink highlighter in continuous circles on the bedsheet, not looking up from it. After about twenty spins, she glanced back at the door. The deadbolt was locked, and the chain was latched. She didn't remember doing that when she'd returned to the room. She stared for another twenty seconds, then turned her gaze to Tony's report.

After taking a sip, Hannah placed the stack on her lap, and began reading it from the first page, searching for anything she might've missed.

FOUR

In the morning, Hannah rolled out of bed and tossed on the same clothes from the previous night. No need to shower. She ate a browning banana, grabbed her backpack, and started to the door, but then stopped, realizing that if something happened to her, no one would know where she was going. That worried her.

She went over to the desk, slid out the top drawer, and retrieved a motel stationery. After tearing out a piece of paper, she began to write:

To whom it may concern, my name is Hannah Jacobs and on 11/11/99, I drove up to Medicine Bow National Forest to hike North Fork trail. My car, a black 1993 Ford Explorer, will be parked at the trailhead. If I don't return by tomorrow, I have gone missing from what I suspect is a serial killer who is responsible for at least six murders, including those of Casey Jacobs and Julia Boone. I've left my files next to the bed.

Hannah positioned the paper in the middle of the desk. Using the TV remote as a paperweight, she placed it at the top of the paper, obscuring the motel logo. As she was closing the door, she looked around the room one more time, having a feeling like she was forgetting something, but she wasn't.

Twenty minutes later, she arrived at a gas station, and as she began filling her tank, her gaze wandered across the street. A patrol car was parked there, in an empty parking lot. The man sitting behind the wheel was Earl, the deputy who had arrested her. He looked straight ahead, avoiding any eye contact with Hannah, as if he were deliberately trying to avoid looking in her direction.

Carefully, Hannah released the handle and hung up the nozzle. Then she walked to the back of her car, slipped between two pumps, and jogged across the street, coming up behind the patrol car. Even when she was standing next to the driver's-side door, Earl didn't look up. Hannah began tapping the window, louder and harder. Finally, after thirty seconds, he rolled down the window.

"Are you following me?" Hannah said.

"I'm doing my job as a Wyoming State Deputy," he said, staring straight ahead, vacant.

"I'm taking that as a yes." She kicked the gravel, creating a small dust cloud. "And just so you know, you're wasting your precious damn time. I'm not doing anything illegal, so fucking stop. And just so you know, I'd prefer to never see your ugly face again."

Hannah turned and started back to the gas station.

"You should stay away from Tony Singleton. That man is nothing but trouble."

Hannah halted, stopping on a dime, then turned around, her anger boiling within. For a moment, she considered grabbing one of the rocks at her feet and hurling it at the police cruiser, but a surge of caution held her back. They wouldn't be as lenient if she was arrested again.

"How long have you been following me asshole?"

"I'm just trying to offer some he—"

"I don't want your fucking help, and I don't need it either!" she yelled, cutting him off.

Finally, he turned to her, his left eyelid twitching as he licked his lips. "You probably should just go home, because I doubt you're going to be able to solve that cold case. I looked at it after you left the station. There was nothing in there but cobwebs, and I'm certain it's never getting solved, especially by someone like you."

"I'm sorry Earl, but just by looking at you I can tell you're pretty dumb, so I don't give a shit about your opinions, especially with regards to that case."

The deputy tipped his hat and smiled. "Have a good day, ma'am. And please stay out of trouble, I would hate to arrest you again."

As he started to roll up the window, Hannah extended her middle finger. Then the patrol car sharply accelerated, leaving the parking lot in a swirl of dust and gravel. The debris hit her legs, but she was unaffected by the sting, staying still until the car disappeared out of sight.

Turning off Highway 130 onto Sand Lake Road, the pavement turned into gravel. It had been at least five miles since Hannah had seen another vehicle, and she was almost certain that she wouldn't see any en route to the trailhead.

About an hour and a half after leaving her motel room, and fifteen minutes after turning off Highway 130, Hannah arrived at the North Fork trailhead parking lot. The last known location of Julia Boone.

Looking at the trail, Hannah remembered Amy Russell,

the final victim of Kevin Strand. Amy had arrived at a trailhead outside of Rocky Mountain National Park to complete a ten-mile hike, but just like Julia, she'd never returned home. Unlike Julia's case, however, Amy's killer was caught, convicted, and sentenced to death, now sitting on death row with an execution date in less than a month. The image of Kevin dead in the execution chamber brought a smile to Hannah's face. She yearned for his death to bring the families closure, just like she yearned to find closure of her own.

As she took the final drags off her cigarette, her thoughts transitioned to Tom Floyd and then finally on to Marshall. What she wouldn't do to have Marshall with her, to be able to ask questions and get his insights.

Hannah stared out the dusty window for a long time. There was nothing but trees and trees reaching the sky for miles.

At the trailhead, a faded information board displayed a map trail along with hiking safety tips, the Fire Danger Rating and types of wildlife one could encounter. Hannah pictured Julia reading the sign before starting on the trail, unaware she'd be dead by morning.

As Hannah began the hike, it started to sleet, and she saw snow patches scattered across the landscape where sunlight couldn't reach. Despite sharing a border, Colorado and Wyoming had distinctly different climates. In November, many parts of Colorado still retained a fall-like atmosphere with mild temperatures, sunny days, and occasional snowfall. Harsher winter conditions typically didn't set in until mid-December or even after Christmas, but in Wyoming, winter arrived early.

As Hannah walked, a leaf fell directly in front of her, and she reached out and caught it. She brought it to her face and rubbed it on her cheek a few times before tilting her head directly back and blowing it behind her.

She knew there wouldn't be an undiscovered clue that she'd miraculously uncover. Part of her had thought that being on the trail and seeing where Julia last walked would give her an epiphany of why this was the abduction site, and the other part thought she'd hike half the day in freezing temperatures and return with nothing but walking pneumonia.

Fallen leaves and broken branches crackled under her feet with nearly every step. She couldn't remember the last time she'd been this isolated. There probably wasn't another person within miles, maybe more. The thought of being this alone, this remote, sent chills down her entire body.

The investigators working Julia's murder couldn't find another person who'd hiked the trail either the day of the abduction or the day before. By all accounts, the only two people on the trail were Julia and the killer.

Hannah stopped, then looked behind her, back down the trail. Not a squirrel, or a chipmunk, or a bird, or any sign of life. Nothing. Turning back, she cupped her mouth and looked skyward.

"Hello!" she screamed. Her voice echoed, and she was somewhat startled at the volume. After ten seconds, she screamed again, this time louder. Her voice vanished into the forest. If Julia had screamed, no one would've heard her.

The investigators also didn't know if she'd been abducted when she arrived at the trailhead, when she returned, or sometime along the hike. There were no drag marks, no signs of a struggle, and her vehicle was untouched, her purse still on the passenger-side floor under a light jacket. It was almost as if she'd been picked up in the forest and dropped lifeless in the park.

Julia wasn't heavy, but she wasn't petite, more of an athletic build at five-eleven and 135 pounds. If she was more than a few hundred yards from the trailhead, he most likely couldn't have carried her out, so he would've had to confront her somewhere near the parking lot, probably at gunpoint, then forced her into his vehicle.

"But why didn't she run?" Hannah whispered.

She thought about that for a long moment. If she was alone in a forest in the middle of nowhere and a man pulled a gun on her, what would she do? Maybe dash up the trail or into the forest.

The trail was an eight-mile out-and-back hike with a fifteen-hundred-foot elevation gain that started at the parking lot, ascended to Lake Solitude, and then returned to the lot, with no connections to any other hikes or roads. Julia had probably known that, and since the parking lot was empty, she would've known there wasn't anyone else on the trail.

Hannah examined the forest. It was eerily quiet, except for the wind swaying the tree branches. The land felt foreboding. And the forest was dense: Douglas fir, ponderosa pine, lodgepole pine, and aspen. Many, many aspen. Escaping off trail would be near impossible and probably result in only two outcomes: becoming lost in the vast wilderness or becoming severely injured and succumbing to exposure.

But once she knew she was being kidnapped, why not fight for her life and leave some sign of a struggle, something to show that she was there, with him in that parking lot? Julia had to know that her chances of survival would plummet to near zero the moment she was in his vehicle, because at that point, her life was 100 percent in his control.

Looking up the trail, Hannah thought about continuing to Lake Solitude for her mental health, but she'd already been hiking for about forty minutes. By her calculations, she'd probably gone about a mile and a half, maybe two, with at least another two to go, then another four from the lake to the parking lot. The day was getting long, and the trees cast long shadows on the trail. At about nine thousand feet, the temperatures were even colder than in Laramie, probably in the mid-forties, and even lower in the shade.

Turning back, Hannah could see over the smaller peaks in the Medicine Bow Mountains and into the Laramie Plains and seemingly on to the grasslands of Kansas. She stared for a second then started down the trail, slowly massaging her frigid nose with her gloved fingers. As she walked, her footsteps seemed loud to her, like a thunderous echo throughout an amphitheater.

About halfway down, Hannah abruptly stopped in the middle of the trail with the stark feeling that someone was watching her. She slid her eyes to her left, then to the right, then back to the left. There was nothing. The seclusion was playing tricks on her.

As she stood motionless, she whispered under her breath, "What if she knew him?"

The day Julia was abducted had been the final night of a waning crescent moon, and maybe he knew this was his last chance at her for at least twenty-six days. Perhaps he'd followed her up to the trailhead and patiently waited for her to return from the hike, isolated from the world, knowing if she screamed pleas for help, they would go unheard. Maybe she didn't see him as a threat, and that might've been why there was no struggle. She wouldn't have known that she was in grave danger until it was too late. Nor would she have grasped how evil he was until she was bound by her wrists and ankles and trapped in his vehicle.

But why did he abduct her from the parking lot instead of her apartment like all the other girls, and why did he leave her body on display in the middle of town? Hannah had an abundance of theories and maybes and questions, but no concrete evidence.

A gust of wind hit her like a punch to the face, making shivers run through her entire body, and only then did she realize just how much the temperature had fallen. Cupping her hands at her mouth, she blew on them for about ten seconds and contemplated jogging the remaining distance to the car, but the last thing she wanted was a twisted ankle.

Some thirty minutes later, she was within eyesight of her vehicle when gunshots rang in the distance. Three quick pops. Hannah stopped, dropped to her knees, and scanned her surroundings, trying to discern where the shots were coming from. Two more shots. Out of nowhere, a flock of birds squawked and flew overhead. Within seconds, they were out of sight.

By her best guess, it sounded far, like it was at least a mile, maybe two, but it was difficult to decipher the origin of the sound as it traveled throughout the mountains. After a long moment, the forest became quiet and very still, and she prayed the shots had come from a mountain range or two over.

Moving cautiously, she continued down the trail, but when she reached the parking lot, she began running. When she got to her car, she took one final long look at the trailhead, then opened the door.

She started the engine and waited almost a full ten seconds before turning the defrost to the highest setting. Once warm air began pushing out the vents, she put the car into gear, but as she pressed on the gas pedal, the engine started to sputter.

"No, no," she said, violently shaking the steering wheel.

Again, she pressed the pedal, this time with a light foot. After a second, the engine turned over and Hannah felt a sense of ease, but then it sputtered again and died. Hannah turned the ignition a dozen times to no avail. Her stomach sank, and a fear that she'd never felt coursed through her body. She was miles from the nearest town, and miles from the nearest phone, and after sunset, the temperatures would begin to drop to below freezing. Part of her wanted to crawl onto the floor board, curl into a ball, and fall asleep. An eternal hibernation.

After wiping away the freezing tears, she attempted to start the car using a multitude of methods. Turning the ignition fast and then holding it for three seconds; turning off the heater, lights, and radio and then turning the ignition slow and easy; pumping the gas pedal and turning the ignition at the exact moment her foot pressed down. She even removed the key and blew on it, just like a Nintendo cartridge, but nothing worked.

If she knew anything about car engines, she would've popped the hood and investigated the issue, but she knew as much about engines as she did about the inner workings of a nuclear submarine. It was pointless to even look.

As she stared out the windshield into the forest and the escaping sun, fog accumulated on the glass. She knew the longer she remained in the car, the colder it would get, the darker it would become, and her odds of her reaching civilization would greatly diminish. Freezing to death was a real possibility.

Glancing down at her watch, she started doing the math. There was about another hour of daylight, followed by about thirty minutes of twilight, then complete and total darkness. It was at least an hour-and-a-half hike on the Sand Lake Road to Highway 130, where she'd most likely have the first chance to flag down a passing vehicle. From the intersection, it was another four miles to Centennial, or a little over an hour on foot if no one picked her up.

At a brisk pace, she could cover the nine miles in about three hours. That would put her arrival sometime around seven. But if she jogged a portion of Sand Creek Road, she could be on the highway before nightfall, and if she continued jogging to Centennial, she could arrive sometime around 5:45. It'd be cold, somewhere in the mid-thirties, but the longer she waited, and the slower she traveled, the colder the night would become.

Hoping for a miracle, Hannah turned the ignition one final time, but nothing. The car didn't make a sound. Dejected, she removed the keys, grabbed the water bottle from the center console, and stuffed them in her backpack, along with her notepad. Then she zipped up her coat, pulled the hoodie over her head, and pulled the trunk latch. She jumped out and rushed to the trunk, then opened the roadside emergency kit, retrieving an extra pair of gloves, an emergency blanket and a miniature flashlight. Unsure if the batteries in the flashlight still worked, Hannah tested it for a few seconds, then shut it off and slid it into her front jean pocket.

She slammed the trunk and examined the endless dirt road below her.

"Think positive thoughts, positive thoughts. Well, it is mostly downhill, with no real elevation climbs. And from the highway, it's only an hour to Centennial."

Bending down, she tied her boots, then sprang up and started jogging without ever looking back.

As Hannah trekked the road, a fog crept down into the range, limiting visibility to around forty feet. It was thick like cotton candy, almost like she could reach out and grab it. Somewhere through the fog, and the snow, and the clouds, was the moon shining down on her. Somewhere.

Unable to continue, Hannah finally stopped. Sucking in the arctic night air, she bent over and placed her hands on her shaking knees, her heart pounding against her chest while her jaw chattered. Snot ran out of her nose and onto her upper lip, and she wiped it with the back of her sleeve.

Standing there in the middle of the dirt road, she realized how cold her toes, and lips, and nose had become. And how tired she was, and how hungry she was, and all she wanted was to sit down for a few minutes, but if she sat down, it'd be difficult to get back up and continue. Hypothermia could come on suddenly, and if she stopped for an extended period, her core temperature could drop to dangerously low levels.

"Come on, you got this—probably already halfway to the highway," she whispered.

Just then, to the south came a howl in the distance, followed by a series of howls that sounded closer. They pierced the night like someone screaming bloody murder. In this region, there were several animals that had been known to kill humans: mountain lions, black bears, moose, and wolves. It was the wolves that really terrified her—on occasions, they'd been known to consume their victims while still alive. Hannah knew animal attacks in Wyoming were rare, but that didn't ease her anxiety.

She listened. The howls faded into a sinister wind. Turning back, she looked down at the seemingly endless winding road, knowing she might never reach the highway. After a deep breath, she knocked the mud off her shoes, took a large drink of water, and continued jogging, her legs burning with every step.

About an hour and fifteen minutes after she left her car, and just as twilight faded, Hannah turned a corner and laid eyes on the highway pavement.

"Yes! Fuck yes!" she screamed, wanting to drop to her knees from exhaustion.

The toughest part of the journey was complete, and it'd only be another hour or so before she was in Centennial, in a motel room with hot water cascading over her entire body. She drank the last few ounces of water, then crossed the highway lines and started jogging east.

After about five minutes, a truck engine roared and broke the silence. The first sign of someone, since she'd driven through Centennial hours ago. Hannah stopped. The engine became louder and louder, and through the fog, the headlights beamed onto the highway.

Carefully, Hannah stepped off the road and onto the shoulder, with one foot partially on the highway and the other at the edge of the embankment. There was a steep drop-off of about thirty feet that only allowed her to saddle the shoulder. Without wasting a moment, she removed the flashlight and began waving it frantically in front of her.

As the truck approached, it slowed and flashed its brights, a signal that the driver had seen her. The brakes produced a high-pitched squeal as the Toyota pickup stopped directly next to Hannah.

Inside the truck was a man, probably closer to fifty than thirty. His hands firmly gripped the steering wheel as he gave Hannah a slow stare. After a moment, he reached across the truck and rolled down the passenger window.

"Darling, what the hell are you doing out here at this time of night? I thought you were a damn deer for a darn minute."

Hannah leaned into the truck. "I did a hike up at North Fork, and when I got back to my car, it wouldn't start. I hiked all the way down from the trailhead and just made it to the road a little bit ago. I'm trying to get to Centennial so I can get a room and go to a garage in the morning."

She studied the man. He was haggard. Soiled clothes, greasy hair, and a smell so vile it was like he'd crawled out of a dumpster. She couldn't get a full read on him, but her instincts were saying he was untrustworthy.

"It's not safe for you to walk on the road—someone's going to come around one of these blind corners and take you out, especially with this fog. People drive like maniacs up around here."

That was a doom Hannah feared. Her mangled body down at the bottom of the embankment.

"Get on in and I'll give you a ride down into town so you can call a mechanic or someone," the driver said. "No one should be out here, especially at night."

Her options were limited. Either climb into the truck with a complete stranger, or walk another hour in near darkness, with frigid temperatures and a high risk of getting hit by a reckless motorist and hurled off the road like an animal.

"Come on, darling, I promise I don't bite," he said with a smile, revealing a mouth of missing teeth.

"You're heading that way, right? I don't want to put you out or anything."

"Yeah, I'm heading down to Laramie to grab some supplies, so it's no problem at all."

"Okay," she said, the trepidation never leaving her voice.

In the truck, the man attempted small talk. His name was George, and he was a Wyoming native. He asked where she was from and what she was doing in Wyoming. She kept her answers short and lied about everything. Her name was Sharon, and she was from Cheyenne, and visiting her boyfriend in Laramie.

"I was supposed to be back at his place an hour ago, so I'm sure he's already worried sick, and probably on his way up here," she said.

All she wanted was for him to stop talking and drive fast, and he did neither.

The sudden fear struck her that the door handles were disabled and she'd be trapped in the truck with no way to escape. Without looking away from the man, she reached for the handle and pulled up, just a touch, not enough to actually open it. It felt like it worked.

"I've lived in this area for twenty years. And I've been all over the good ol' United States, and there is no place I'd rather live than right here. This is God's country, if you ask me."

"Yeah, it's beautiful," she muttered.

"I actually have this nice little cabin up the road. It's not much, but it's near the top of Barrett Ridge and overlooks the entire forest."

"That's nice."

After a momentary lull, the man placed his hand on Hannah's thigh.

"Would you be interested in coming over for some fun?" George said.

She yanked his hand away and leaned into the door panel. Countless scenarios began running through her head. *Did he have a gun or some type of weapon? Was he going to kidnap her? Had he followed her to the trailhead and tampered with her car? Could this be the man who killed Julia?*

The cabin felt like it was closing in on her.

Hannah started doing the calculations in her head. If she jumped out of the truck doing forty and executed a perfect tuck and roll onto the pavement, she might get up with a few minor cuts and bumps. That was a big if, and highly unlikely. More out of a movie than real life.

Odds were she'd land hard and break something or knock herself out, and she'd be in a worse position than she was now. Injured or unconscious, and the man would be in complete control.

With every ounce of courage, Hannah squared her shoulders to the man. Leaning as far back into the door as possible, she wrapped her right fingers around the door handle.

"If you touch me again, I promise I'll break every fucking finger in your hand," she said, her voice growing louder with each word.

"Easy sweetheart, no need to get upset. I just thought since I'm doing you a favor, you could return one to me."

"Just shut the fuck up and drive! Don't say another word!" she screamed. "And don't you dare look at me again."

For the next twenty-five minutes, the truck was silent. Not for a second did she take her eyes off George, and he never looked back at her. Those were some of the longest minutes of her life.

Then, like an oasis, the city lights of Centennial appeared out of the corner of her eye. For the first time in hours, she exhaled a sigh of relief.

At the first stop sign in town, Hannah said, "Let me out here."

The truck jerked to a stop, and she jumped out and slammed the door behind her. The man yelled something, but his voice was drowned out by the truck's engine. From the sidewalk, she watched until the taillights disappeared into the night.

Across the street was the Wyoming Motel, a single-story building with a dirt parking lot surrounded by what looked like ten rooms. There were two cars in the parking lot and a neon sign in the office window that flashed "Vacancy."

A bell chimed as Hannah walked into the front office. The clerk, a man probably in his twenties, glanced up from a magazine as she approached the counter. Next to him was a stereo playing "Drain You" by Nirvana at a low volume.

"How can I help you tonight?" the man said.

"I'd like a room for the night."

"Perfect. Do you want the honeymoon or the penthouse suite?"

"Listen, I'm in no mood for any of your cute fucking jokes. I just want a room that has a working TV and a phone, and preferably one that is close to the lobby."

"Well, you're in luck. Room number one is available, and it's that beauty right next door," the man said, pointing to the room next to the office.

Hannah didn't take her eyes off of him. "That'll work."

"Perfect. It'll be $29 plus tax. Will that be cash or credit?"

"Cash."

"Okay, I'll just need you to fill out this registration form."

Hannah made up an address in Laramie and a phone number with a 307 area code, and signed the form as Tiffany Barnes. That was her standard name when getting a motel room that allowed cash payments.

Reaching into her purse, she removed her wallet and handed the man two twenties. He handed back the change and the room key.

"Have a good night, and don't hesitate to give me a buzz if you need anything. Just press zero and that'll ring to me."

"Actually, would you happen to have a map of Laramie or Wyoming?" Hannah said, glancing behind the counter.

"Nah, I don't, but unless someone tore it out, there should be one in the back of the Yellow Pages. It should be in one of the nightstand drawers."

Hannah thanked him, then turned and walked out of the lobby.

In the room, she pulled the curtain tight and turned on the overhead light, then both lamps. Grabbing the remote, she flipped on the TV and pressed mute. Like a child scared of the dark, she wanted the room to be as bright as possible.

Dropping to her knees, she checked under the bed. Next, she inspected the bathroom and behind the shower curtain. Then she sat still on the edge of the bed, listening. Dead quiet. For almost five minutes, she watched the door. Nothing.

She pushed herself up, tripled-checked the locked door, then walked into the bathroom and slipped out of her clothes. Her toes and fingers were still freezing. This always happened after an extended time in cold weather, and the only way to warm up her extremities was a long, near-scalding shower. She turned the handle to hot, then slipped into the bathtub, and remained in the tub until the water became lukewarm.

After drying off and getting dressed, she pulled her notepad and pen out of her backpack, then reached across the bed and removed the phone book from the bottom drawer. In the back was a detailed colored map of Cheyenne, Casper, and Laramie, as well as a full-page map of Wyoming with major cities, major tourist attractions, and highways and interstates. With her index finger, she drew a circle around Laramie and studied the map.

Out of the corner of her eye, she noticed a cut on the back of her forearm that was bleeding. She examined it for a moment. Maybe a branch in the forest or something in the man's truck? Nonchalantly, she wiped the blood on her pants.

Julia had left her house at around one, arrived at

the trailhead sometime around two thirty, and been abducted sometime between three and six. She'd been discovered at six the next morning. A total of twelve to fifteen hours in captivity. For the other murders, the killer averaged about two to four hours with each victim in their apartments, but since he spent more time with Julia, maybe the murder occurred at his house or mobile home or RV or semi-truck.

He also would've had to be very familiar with Laramie, because he was confident enough that he'd go unnoticed and undetected while placing a dead body on a bench in a park in the middle of town that was less than ten blocks from the Albany Police Department.

In a steady rhythm, Hannah tapped the map for another minute. "He fucking lives in Laramie," she whispered. "And he lived there when he killed Casey."

After Casey's murder, he must've moved to northern Wyoming to stalk his next victims. Then, once enough time had passed and he deemed it was safe, he returned to his original hunting grounds and decided Julia would be his next prey. He probably knew her from the bank or saloon, maybe a customer or someone who'd admired her from a distance.

Hannah ripped out the map, folded it in half, and stuck it in her backpack, then climbed into bed. It'd been a long day, and she was exhausted.

As she closed her eyes, the sound of a semi-truck engine resonated throughout the room, shaking the walls. The engine sounded like it was about to drive through the front door, and the high beams shined through the curtains and onto the wall like a police helicopter spotlight. Hannah sat up and waited until the sound of the engine faded.

That night she slept poorly, but that was something she was accustomed to—most nights drifting in and out of sleep and jolting herself back awake. Never sleeping for more than a few hours at a time. Lucid dreams and vivid nightmares invading her subconscious mind. Mostly nightmares.

Sunlight beaming through the curtains woke her. Springing up, she glanced at the clock radio on the nightstand. It was 8:53.

"Damn it," she muttered.

Hannah wanted to wake up at 7:45, so she could grab a coffee and arrive at the mechanic when they opened, but she'd forgotten to set the alarm. Jumping out of bed, she threw on her clothes, snagged her backpack, and rushed out of the room.

Country Gas and Auto was the only service station in Centennial, located just four blocks from the motel. There were four gas pumps out front and a tow truck parked on the side of the building. It looked closed, but Hannah could see someone reading a newspaper inside.

As she pushed the door open, a bell chimed and the man behind the counter leisurely glanced up from the paper and nodded. A radio behind him was on a sports station, and the hosts were discussing the University of Wyoming football team and their most recent loss.

"What can I do for you, darling?" he said as Hannah approached the counter.

"I was wondering if I could get a tow from North Fork trailhead," she said, somewhat embarrassed. She told him her car died at the parking lot, and she hitched a ride into town, but deliberately omitted the investigation into Julia's murder.

"What the hell were you doing up there alone? You know a girl got murdered up there last spring and it's still unsolved?"

"No, I didn't know that," she said, her tone casual.

The man closed the paper, dropped it on the floor, and got up.

"Any idea what's wrong with it?"

Hannah shrugged. "I don't know anything about cars. All I know is when I turned the key, nothing happened. Not a single noise."

He stared at her for a moment, with the kind of disapproving look a parent would give to a child.

"Let me grab my toolbox and I'll meet you outside in a couple minutes."

Ten minutes later, they were in the tow truck, heading west on Highway 130 toward Sand Lake Road.

"I'm Larry, by the way," he said, not taking his eyes off the road.

Hannah turned to him and smiled. "Nice to meet you, Larry. I'm Hannah."

Gingerly, the man scratched his beard. "I'm still trying to figure out what you were doing up here."

"I just wanted to be in the mountains one last time before winter, so I decided to come up here to do a hike," Hannah said, stringing together the words.

"I've lived in this area my entire life, and people don't decide to come up here on a whim in the middle of November, unprepared. Hardcore enthusiasts, yes, but not day hikers."

"I swear, I've heard great things about this area so I thought I'd check it out."

Larry lowered the radio volume. "Hannah, I didn't just fall off the turnip truck. So, you're either as dumb as a bag of rocks, or you're full of shit." He glanced at her. "And you don't look that dumb, so I'd guess you're full of shit. Am I right?"

"Yeah, I'm full of shit," she said.

"That's what I thought," he said with a chuckle. "So,

what really brought you up here?"

"I'm investigating the murder of Julia Boone, the girl who was abducted from North Fork in May."

"Julia Boone," he said, then repeated her name at a whisper. "That's a damn shame what happened to her. It was like she vanished into thin air." He paused for a moment, gathering his thoughts. "My parents moved to Wyoming over forty years ago to get away from big-city violence, but now it's in my backyard. I guess no place is safe anymore."

Hannah was about to say something, but she stopped. She could see on his face that he was sorry for asking. Without saying another word, she knew he didn't want to talk about the evil that had happened in these mountains, mere miles from the safety of his home. For the rest of the drive, they had minimal conversation, and a little over an hour after leaving Centennial, they arrived at the North Fork trailhead parking lot. A light snow had started to fall.

"You're lucky you didn't get caught up here today— we're supposed to get three to four inches starting this afternoon," Larry said.

"Yeah, that wouldn't have been good," Hannah said, watching a dusting of snowflakes accumulate on her jacket.

After retrieving the toolbox, Larry instructed her to get into the driver's seat and pop the hood. Then he began inspecting the engine compartment.

"Try to start it!" he shouted.

Hannah turned the key, but there was nothing. Larry told her to try it again, and she did but with the same results.

"Everything looks good here," he said, spitting next to the front tire. He removed a flashlight from his front pocket and dropped to his knees, crawling under the car.

"Bingo! I think I found the problem."

"What is it?" Hannah said.

"See that right there?" he said, pointing to the gravel next to the driver's-side front tire. "That is gasoline."

Larry grabbed a handful of the soaked gravel and smelled it to confirm his assumption. He nodded feverishly, then offered the gravel toward Hannah to smell. She politely declined.

"Umm, okay. Could you please elaborate how gas is on the ground and not in my engine?"

"Well, there are a handful of possibilities, but 95 percent of the time it's because there was some sort of tear in the gas line."

"What is the other 5 percent?"

"Someone deliberately cuts it."

"A cut?"

"Yeah, I've seen it a couple of times, but this doesn't really look like one."

Dropping to his knees, he let out a loud sigh and then crawled under the car again.

"Yeah, this is most likely a tear. And it had to happen somewhere close, or else you would've run out of gas long before you made it up here. Did you run over any rocks, or branches or anything that could've scratched the undercarriage?

"I don't remember. Perhaps," she said, shrugging.

After a minute, he crawled out from under the car and stood up, then started brushing off the dirt.

"I'll tow it back to the shop and get it on the lift and patch it up. It should be as good as new and I'll have you on your way in like two hours. Maybe three tops."

As he started back to the tow truck, Hannah said, "Larry, do you think someone could've cut it to make it look like it was ripped on something?"

He thought for a moment, stroking his beard. "I guess

that could be a possibility, but they would've had to follow you all the way up here and wait until you were on the hike."

"Yeah," she muttered, "he'd have to be very patient."

FIVE

alking on the sidewalk to the Holt house, the sun weaved in and out of the clouds as the power lines dangled from house to house, countless strings of aluminum humming a quiet buzz, carrying thousands of volts of electricity.

Looking at the power lines, Hannah recalled a newspaper article about a newlywed couple on a walk when a line snapped and landed on the feet of the husband, electrocuting him in seconds. The wife instinctively reached for him, attempting to pull him back, but she became part of the electrical circuit. They both died instantly. When first responders found them, the bodies were charred to a crisp.

Since reading that story, Hannah kept an eye out for power lines that crossed her path. That, along with avoiding cracks in the sidewalk, kept her preoccupied on simple walks through any neighborhood.

Without realizing it, she found herself standing in front of the home of the second address with the Holt last name from the White Pages. Before leaving the motel, she'd called both numbers. The first number was a lovely lady named Peggy who lived with her cat Sophie and didn't have children and wasn't related to nor did she know anyone named Stacy. The second number, the house she was now in front of, hadn't answered. Hannah had called three times within an hour and gotten the answering machine every time.

Glancing down at her notepad, Hannah confirmed that the address she'd written was the one on the front door. She stared at the house for a long moment. It was a single-story ranch house in the northeast section of Laramie, seemingly the only affluent neighborhood in town. Perfectly manicured lawn and landscaping, two newer cars in the driveway and a basketball hoop above the garage. It reminded her of the first house she'd lived in. Long before her parents got divorced, long before her dad became an alcoholic—and long before Casey was murdered.

Walking up the pathway to the front door, Hannah pondered what she would say if anyone answered, if she'd lie or tell the truth, use her real name or one of her many aliases. Finally, she decided her name was Rachel and she went to UW with Stacy, and she was in town for a couple of days and wanted to see if Stacy wanted to grab lunch. If she was pressed for further details, she'd make it up on the fly.

As Hannah reached for the doorbell, the front door flung open and a woman wearing a bathrobe and slippers glared at her.

With a hollow voice, the woman said, "How can I help you?"

Momentarily startled, Hannah was at a loss for words. "I was wondering if Stacy is home?" she managed to get out.

A small dog barked from another room. The woman

ignored the dog and peered at Hannah with hardened eyes.

"I'm sorry, but I can't help you. It's been months since I've seen or talked to her."

The woman took a step back and started closing the door. Hannah placed her palm on the door and stopped it, leaving about a three-inch opening.

"Please, I really just want to talk to her. Do you have her number?" Hannah said.

"Like I said, I haven't talked to her in months, and I don't even know how to reach her. Now, please get off my property before I have to call the authorities."

Hannah removed her hand, barely escaping the door slamming shut. She could hear the deadbolt turn, and a few seconds later the dog stopped barking.

As she was walking back along the pathway to the sidewalk a man, probably in his early twenties, appeared from the side of the house holding a torque wrench, hands covered in grease.

"What do you want with Stacy?" the man said.

"I'm an old friend from school and just wanted to reconnect."

The man looked Hannah up and down. "I call bullshit. I might not have been super close with my sis, but I knew most of her friends and I've never seen your face before."

Fleetingly, Hannah contemplating continuing with the lie or telling the truth.

"Okay. My name is Hannah Jacobs, and I'm a private investigator. I'm trying to solve the murder of my sister, and I think the man who killed her also killed Julia Boone. And I think Julia might've known the killer. I just want to talk to your sister and ask some questions. Maybe Julia said something to her."

The man tapped the wrench against his thigh, and one eyebrow rose. He removed a cigarette pack from out of his front pocket and flipped the lid in one motion. Then he brought the pack to his mouth and pulled a cigarette out with his lips.

"Got a light?"

Hannah walked to him, lighting his cigarette and then one for herself. Peering down, she saw three pairs of infant footprints in the cement. Remnants of a happier time, an optimistic time.

"Come on, let's take a walk. I don't want Mama seeing us talking out here," the man said, gesturing to the house. "I'm Tim by the way, Stacy's kid brother."

They walked in silence for a bit, and then the man spoke. "Everything that happened to Julia really spooked Stacy. I mean, I don't blame her, but she is a completely different person since it happened. It's like I'm talking to someone who isn't my sister, you know?"

"I understand," Hannah said. "Did you ever try to talk to her about it?"

"I tried, but after the funeral, she just locked herself in her apartment and didn't really say much of anything. I called nearly every day for weeks, and I'd say the most I ever got out of her was probably twenty words." He took a quick drag. "Then one day she tells us she's moving to Billings."

"Montana?"

"Yeah. That surprised the hell outta me. I had no idea that she knew anyone up there, but I guess this guy Bobby she met at UW lives there. I hung out with him a handful of times. He was a nice guy, almost too nice, and kinda nerdy. She always liked the bad boys, so I was really surprised when I heard that was who she was moving in with."

"When was the last time you talked to her?"

He took a pull off the cigarette. "August. She called on my birthday, but that was only for a couple of minutes."

"You haven't seen or talked to her in four months?"

"Not a single word," the man said, drawing out the words.

"Do you think she is in danger?" Hannah said.

"Nah, I think after Julia was murdered, and it not getting solved, she is done with this town, and this fucking state. I wouldn't be surprised if she never moved back here again."

"Would it be possible to get her number?" Hannah said.

"If I had it, I'd give it to you, but she says she doesn't have a home phone. And when she calls, it's always from a payphone."

"What if you need to get hold of her?"

"We are shit out of luck."

"I guess you don't have her address then."

"Nope. All I know is that she lives in an apartment somewhere in Billings with Bobby. And the last time I talked to her she was working full-time at an Albertsons in the produce department and part-time at a Dairy Queen." Tim chuckled. "She has a degree in nursing and she's working at a fucking Dairy Queen, making blizzards and shit. Not really what I envisioned my sister doing with her life."

Tim dropped the cigarette onto the sidewalk, then smashed it with his boot. He turned to Hannah.

"You really think you know who killed Julia?" he said.

"I don't know. I might have a lead, and that's why I wanna talk to your sister. It's a long shot, but it might be something."

Tim adjusted the bill of his cap. "Well, that's more than these shit-for-brains cops up here have found, so you're already one up on them." He spat. "I probably should get going. I'm sure Mama saw me walking off with you, and she's probably moments from losing her shit. She hasn't been herself since Stacy left. I think it broke her. She'll fly off the handle if I leave a dirty dish in the sink."

"It's fine," Hannah said, extending her hand. "Thank you for all your help."

He shook it. "Are you really going up to Billings to try to find Stacy?"

"Yeah, I am."

"Well good luck, and if you find her, tell her I miss her."

Hannah smiled, nodded, and continued on the sidewalk, avoiding every crack.

Later that afternoon, she parked in Tony's apartment complex. Sitting in the car, she leaned back into the headrest and methodically smoked a cigarette.

When she'd returned to Laramie from Centennial, Hannah realized she didn't have anyone to tell about what had happened at the trailhead. There was no way in hell she was going to the police, and she didn't know a single other person in town except for Tony.

Being alone was something she had grown accustomed to, but it never got any easier. For years, Marshall had been her go-to confidant, but since his death, she had no one. Not a single person.

After the final drag, Hannah stabbed the cigarette into the ashtray, grabbed her coat, and started across the parking lot. At the front door, she knocked three times, softly, then waited. Moments later, she knocked again, a little harder.

The door opened. Tony was standing in the entryway

with a smile on his face like he'd been expecting her arrival.

"Is this a bad time?" Hannah asked, cursing herself for not calling first.

"No, no. Come on in," Tony said, gesturing her inside.

The apartment smelled of marijuana and sex. Hannah looked around, expecting someone to appear from the bedroom, but there was no one. She sat on the couch, picked up a throw pillow, and wrapped her arms around it like she was squeezing a teddy bear.

"Is everything okay?" he said.

"So, yesterday I went to Medicine Bow, the trail where Julia was reported missing. I hiked up a few miles, turned around, and when I got back to my car, it wouldn't start. I almost got stranded up there."

"Whoa, back up a second. What were you doing up there?"

"I honestly don't know. I just wanted to see it with my own eyes. See what Julia saw before she was murdered."

"And you went up there alone?" Tony said.

Hannah nodded.

"Girl, you got to be more careful. It's no joke up there, especially this time of year. If the elements or a serial killer don't kill you, a bear probably will."

"I know. It was very dumb."

Hannah was embarrassed. She felt like a greenhorn for putting herself in such a vulnerable situation.

"What was wrong with your car?"

"The mechanic said a tear in the fuel line. It probably got snagged on a rock or a branch on the drive up to the trailhead." She paused, her breath catching in her throat. "But he also said there was a small chance it could've been cut."

"Cut?" Tony glanced at her sideways. "Do you think anyone fucked with your car while you were hiking?"

Hannah remained quiet for a bit, then mumbled, "That is a possibility."

"Damn Hannah, you can't do that shit. Someone might be following you."

She knew that. That was all she'd been able to think about after the rush faded and she was lying in the motel bed, staring at the ceiling. She slept with one eye open and sprang to attention at any slight sound. She was certain the apprehension would last as long as she was in Wyoming, and she feared that it would persist even when she returned to Denver. The man was a serial killer who wasn't afraid to travel. What would stop him from following her home and breaking into her apartment while she slept?

"I know," Hannah said.

"So how the fuck did you get out of there?"

Hannah told him about the events that had transpired the previous night—the walk on the highway in the dark, the ride with the old man in the truck, the motel in Centennial. Finally, she told him about her theory that the killer could be living within the Laramie city limits.

"Are you serious?" Tony said.

Hannah nodded with a touch of excitement in her face. "And that's kinda why I'm here. I was wondering if you could set up a meeting with your friend who works down at the courthouse."

Tony reached for a pack of cigarettes on the coffee table, flipped the lid with his thumb, removed a joint, and lit it, taking a hit. Then he offered it to Hannah.

"No, I'm good," she said.

"And what exactly would you like to talk to him about?"

"I want a list of all Ford F-150s manufactured from 1975 to 1997 that are registered in Albany County, as well as Carbon, Platte, and Laramie."

Tony took another hit, then tilted his head back and blew the smoke to the ceiling. "You know you're going to get a list as long as the phone book. Half the state drives an F-150."

"Yes, I've heard. But that, along with sex, age, and marital status, should narrow it down quite a bit."

Tony started nodding slowly. "Okay, I see what you're doing. That makes a lot of sense." He let out a long exhale. "My friend is always a little apprehensive about doing these types of favors, but let me work some magic. I'll give him a call later tonight."

"You're amazing."

"I know."

Hannah smiled. "And by the way, I'm going to Billings tomorrow morning to try to find Stacy Holt."

Tony's eyes widened. "You're going where? For what?"

At a slower cadence, Hannah repeated herself.

"Oh, I heard you the first time. I just don't know why the fuck you're going to look for her."

"I have a feeling Julia might've known the killer," she said.

"For real?"

Hannah nodded. "Yeah, something spooked Stacy enough to pack up and move her life to Montana. Maybe she knew who it was, and instead of going to the cops, she thought she'd be safer disappearing into another state. I need to know why she left."

After another hit and a slight cough, Tony said, "Do you want me to go with you?"

"No, I'll be fine, I promise. I just need you to sweet-talk your friend and get that vehicle registration list."

"It's as good as gotten, honey."

The next morning, Hannah showered, dressed, and threw two changes of clothes into a backpack. An old coffee maker and basket of instant coffee sat on the dresser, along with various packets of sugar and creamer. Ripping open a packet of coffee, she dumped it into the machine and pressed brew. Brown, caffeinated water wasn't ideal, but it would do in a pinch.

With the coffee cup in hand and backpack over her shoulder, she closed the door, checked the lock three times, then went downstairs and grabbed an apple from a basket at the front desk.

The drive to Billings was a little over six hours, and her itinerary was to drive on Highway 487 for 150 miles to Casper, getting there around noon. Refuel and grab a quick snack, then start on I-25 and drive another hundred miles to Buffalo, get gas there, and then travel the last 160 miles to Billings.

If everything went to plan, she'd arrive sometime around four. Then she'd get a room, shower, and begin the search. There were four Albertsons and three Dairy Queens in Billings, and Hannah was going to start at the closest one to the motel, then branch out until she located Stacy.

A rush of anxiety overcame her as she thought about everything that could go wrong: a flat tire, engine troubles, running out of gas, driving into a snow storm, or taking a wrong turn and getting lost. Placing her left index and middle finger onto her right wrist, she closed her eyes and started taking deep breaths. An anxiety attack was never far away.

"Calm down. Everything is going to be fine," she whispered to herself.

The route was on major highways and interstates that

were moderately trafficked. If anything happened, there would be passing motorists who'd be able to assist her.

For another two minutes, she kept her eyes closed while focusing on her breathing. After her pulse lowered, Hannah reached for her CD book, flipping the pages until she located *OK Computer* by Radiohead. Removing the CD, she blew on it for good luck then buffed it on her shirt. She slipped it into the CD player and skipped to track number ten, "No Surprises." That song was her quick-release Xanax. After listening to it once, she started it over, then pulled the gear shift into drive and pulled out of the Motel 6 parking lot.

The landscape along Highway 487 was desolate. To the west lay open fields with countless round hay bales; to the east a barbwire fence that ran parallel with miles of the highway. Off in the distance, a "Dole for President" sign stood in an open field, the colors fading from years of harsh weather.

With one hand on the steering wheel, Hannah used her free hand to flip through pages of the CD book on the passenger seat. On the fourth page was a CD with black Sharpie titled "Mix Disc #4." The writing on the disc was hers, but she had no memory of making it. She pulled it out of the sleeve then slid it into the stereo.

The first song was "Lovesong" by The Cure. The moment the bass line echoed throughout her car, she got shivers and was transformed back to 1992 and being nineteen, and sitting in a Ford Ranger with a boy named Daniel in the Green Mountain parking lot overlooking Denver.

Until that night, she'd only heard one song off *Disintegration,* and after Daniel swore it was one of the best albums ever recorded, they listened to it from front to back, mostly in silence, watching the city lights twinkle like stars in the sky while passing a joint back and forth. After the album ended, they started it over and made love in the cab of the truck for what seemed like hours. Hannah had thought he was the one; she always thought the man she was involved with was the one.

For two months that summer, they were each other's world. Talking every day, hanging out every night, sleeping together at every opportunity they had and experiencing the best hiking excursion of her life, Bear Lake to Grand Lake in Rocky Mountain National Park.

Then one day it was over. No breakup, no fights, no yelling, no tears, and no long, drawn-out goodbye. Thinking back, Hannah couldn't remember what ended the relationship. Maybe some were just never meant to last.

After that summer, they saw each other a handful of times at the occasional party. They'd make small talk, then go their separate ways. Last she'd heard, he'd enlisted in the Army and been deployed overseas: Iraq, Kuwait, somewhere in the Middle East. She'd probably never speak to him again, and that brought a wave of melancholy.

It'd only been seven years, but it felt like a lifetime. Nineteen to twenty-six. Back then, she was naive and still hopeful for what the future held. Over the years, she'd forgotten names, and faces, and places, but every time she heard a song off that album, she was reminded of the night on Green Mountain, and that summer with Daniel.

When the song finished, Hannah pressed the back button and turned up the volume. The louder the music, the faster she drove, approaching ninety, the dashed yellow lines becoming almost solid.

With care, she bit her fingernails on her right hand, spitting the tiny pieces out the crack in the window. It was a habit she despised, but it was something she couldn't stop—almost as hard as quitting smoking. Sometimes she bit her nails so low that they bled, and required a band-aid to stop the bleeding, as well as to provide pressure and alleviate the pain.

At a gas station in Casper, she pulled in next to a pump, refueled then went into the station and walked up to the counter. An old man sat in a chair behind the cash register, spitting sunflower seeds into a plastic cup, listening to a talk show on AM radio. He wore a faded shirt that read "World's Best Husband." Hannah stared at the shirt for a moment and questioned the validity of the statement.

"$22.56 on pump three."

"Okey dokie. One second," he said, pressing buttons on the register.

His face was weathered, and his nose was red and swollen. Probably too many cigarettes, too much whiskey. A long, hard life.

The talk show was discussing Y2K. He glanced over his shoulder and listened for a moment, then looked back at Hannah.

"What do you think of this Y2K stuff?"

"I honestly don't know much about it, so I really don't have an opinion."

"You should—it could be the start of Armageddon," he said somewhat excitedly.

All Hannah wanted was to pay for the gas and be on her way, but some people needed to talk the ear off of every person they encountered. Not Hannah. She preferred a smile and minimal conversation.

The man continued, "They say all the computers weren't programmed to update to the year 2000, so all the flights, and banking systems, and power grids might stop working at 12:01 on January 1. It could really fuck shit up. I've been thinking about taking my money out of the bank. It's not much, but it's all I got. Just to make sure I have cash if everything goes sideways."

Y2K was the furthest thing from her mind, but in some ways, she would welcome a complete collapse of civilization. A reset for every living person.

"I guess I should also take my money out of the bank and hide it under my mattress."

"Is that your attempt at humor, little lady? I can tell you what, when the day of reckoning comes, there'll be three types of people. The wealthy ones, the ones who prepared, and the ones who thought that day would never come. I can tell you're not wealthy, so I'll assume you're one of the skeptical ones? Well, I wish you all the best, because life will not be easy once it comes."

Cocking her head to the left, Hannah said, "Can I just pay for my gas and get on my way?"

The old man muttered something under his breath before taking her money.

A little over two hours later, the "Welcome to Montana" sign was in sight, and as Hannah crossed the state border, she realized it was the farthest north she'd ever been. Hell, besides a handful of trips to her grandma's house in Orlando as a kid, she'd never really ventured outside of the borders of Colorado or Wyoming. A trip to Garden City, Kansas, for a cousin's wedding when she was thirteen and a weeklong camping trip to the Black Hills and Mount Rushmore—that was it.

Right then she decided that when she returned to Denver, she was going to plan a vacation. Maybe Alaska, maybe Iceland. No, somewhere warm with a beach and tropical drinks full of rum and pineapple.

After checking in to the motel, Hannah sat at the edge of the bed and turned on the TV and started aimlessly flipping through the channels. For about five minutes, she thought about taking a quick shower, but decided against it. She knew it'd be a long, hot shower, and that would turn into crawling under the sheets and falling asleep for a few hours. She wanted to begin searching for Stacy immediately—she didn't want to spend a minute more in Billings than she had to.

Hannah drove to the Albertsons about a mile away and spoke to three employees. The first two said they'd never heard of Stacy, and the last one, a kid who looked like he was sixteen, said he could find Stacy if she bought him a case of beer. Hannah politely told him to fuck off.

At the second store, she spoke to another trio of employees, but again, none of them knew Stacy. Walking back to her car, she decided to try the Dairy Queen about a half mile away, and if Stacy wasn't there, she'd return to the motel, pass out for the night, and try the final four locations the following morning.

Across the street from the Dairy Queen, about forty kids were clustered around a stack of wood pallets in the parking lot of Billings West High School. Most of them were arm in arm, chanting something that Hannah couldn't make out, their voices obscured by the distance. She watched for a minute or so, then entered the Dairy Queen.

Inside were two employees, a young man probably not out of high school standing at the cash register and a woman in her mid to late twenties, hopefully Stacy, working the drive-through window. An older couple sat in a booth toward the back of the restaurant, both feverishly licking ice cream cones. In unison, they looked up at Hannah as she walked in, staring for a moment before returning to the ice cream.

As Hannah stepped up to the counter, the kid looked up at her with a vacant face, probably high.

"What can I get for you tonight?" he said.

"Is that Stacy Holt?" Hannah asked, pointing to the girl.

"It is."

"Could you grab her for me?"

"Umm, sure."

The kid walked to the drive-through window and began talking to the girl. Glancing back, she studied Hannah for a long moment. Finally, she shuffled to the counter.

The girl smelled of cigarettes and French fries. Up close, she looked frail, and even though she was at least three inches taller, she probably weighed less than Hannah. Perhaps an eating disorder. If Hannah hadn't known her age, she would've guessed that she was a teenager. It was probably how people perceived Hannah in return.

"Do I know you?" she said. Her voice sounded like that of a young girl.

"I was wondering if I could talk to you about Julia Boone?"

"Julia." The girl sighed, seeming lost in a memory for a moment. Then she spoke again, nervous. "Why are you here?" Large black bags rested under her defeated eyes. Probably not a decent night's sleep since Julia's murder.

Hannah took the girl's arm, leaned in, and whispered, "My sister was killed by the same man a decade before Julia."

"Bullshit."

"Casey Jacobs. At the Sage Creek apartments in Laramie in 1989. Since Casey, I believe he has murdered at least five other girls including Julia, and he will not stop until he is caught. And I promise I wouldn't be here, but I think Julia might've known the killer."

A long silence followed, broken by the kid when he dropped an empty dishwashing rack. It hit the tile, producing a jarring bang. Both Hannah and Stacy looked in that direction, then after a moment turned back to each other.

"There's a bench out front. Give me twenty minutes to close down the store and I'll meet you out there," Stacy said.

Outside the Dairy Queen, the crowd in the school parking lot had seemingly doubled or tripled. Hannah sat on the bench and watched their every movement. They sang louder and louder, and she surmised it was the school fight song.

At the conclusion of the song, the crowd stopped moving, and the night stood completely silent. Then, like a fireball, the pallets burst into an inferno. Hannah jolted back—even at a distance of about a few hundred feet, she could feel the heat against her face. The crowd cheered and began throwing branches, boards and anything flammable into the bonfire. The chaotic flames grew to heights of thirty or forty feet, and Hannah became spellbound watching them dance in the night sky.

"Jesus, I need to move out of this hick town," Stacy muttered.

Startled, Hannah jerked around, "Fuck, you scared the shit out of me."

"Sorry, I should've said something."

"It's fine. I was just enthralled with these little pyros." Turning back to the crowd, Hannah said, "Do you know what the hell is going on with their séance?"

"Well, it's the end of the high school football season and that's how these rednecks celebrate. And I guess since I live in this godforsaken town, that makes me a redneck as well." She shook her head. "C'mon, let's go to my place to talk. I feel safer there. It's only about five blocks from here, so we can just walk."

On the walk to the apartment, they chatted nonchalantly, with Stacy mostly dominating the conversation. How much she despised her jobs, how much she wanted out of Montana and where Hannah was from.

"Do you like Denver?" Stacy said.

"It's okay. I mean I've never lived outside of Colorado, so I can't really gauge it against anything else."

"I always kinda thought I'd end up in Denver someday, but never Montana." She chuckled. "I guess there certainly are worse places than Billings, but I can tell you one thing—if you're hungry after ten o'clock, you're pretty much shit out of luck."

At the front door of the apartment, Stacy turned back to Hannah. "Just so you know, the guy I live with is home, but we can go into the bedroom and he'll leave us alone."

Hannah nodded.

Inside the apartment, sitting in a bean bag in the middle of the living room was a tall, lanky man playing a video game and listening to "Three Days" by Jane's Addiction.

"Bobby, this is Hannah, an old friend from Laramie," Stacy said.

"Nice to meet you," he said, glancing over his shoulder.

"It's nice to meet you as well."

Then there was an uncomfortable moment of silence, like everyone wanted to say something but nobody did.

Finally, Stacy said, "We're gonna go into the bedroom and catch up."

"Okay babe, let me know if you guys need anything," Bobby said before returning his attention to the TV and unpausing the game.

"Would you like something to drink?" Stacy said.

Hannah nodded politely. "Sure."

"I have to clean a couple glasses, so I'll meet you in

the bedroom. It's the second door on the left," Stacy said, pointing toward the hallway.

The bedroom was clean and tidy; the bed was made, and not a single piece of clothing was out of place. A bowl on the dresser contained potpourri that emitted a lavender scent. Hannah sat at the edge of the bed, and within a minute, Stacy entered the room, locked the door, then handed a plastic gas station cup to Hannah and sat next to her.

"Sorry, I'm out of soda, so I hope this is okay—it's strawberry," the girl said.

"This is perfect."

They each took a sip. Hannah couldn't remember the last time she'd drank Kool-Aid. It had probably been at least a decade, maybe more. It reminded her of being a kid, running free with her sister until the streetlights came on. Hannah took another sip.

Staring blankly forward, Stacy said, "Bobby is very nice, and he listened to me after Julia died. Like really listened, you know? He said I could move up here and live rent free, and I didn't want to stay in Laramie, so I jumped at the chance. I packed up and was gone a couple weeks after the funeral." She took a quick sip. "I call him my boyfriend, but he's more like a roommate. He'd rather play video games than have sex. But I'm okay with that, because I'd rather masturbate than sleep with him."

They both laughed. Hannah sensed that since Julia's death, Stacy didn't have anyone to confide in. She knew that feeling all too well.

Hannah had always considered herself a good listener, maybe even great. The shoulder to cry on. It was something that she attributed to being an introvert. The problem with the majority of people was that when someone else was talking, they weren't actually listening, just waiting for the opportunity to talk themselves. But not Hannah—she listened to every word and never wasted one herself.

"This town is a slow death sentence. Every day it gets darker and darker, and every night it gets longer and colder. I guess until one day you wake up and you're seventy with one foot in the grave. Well not me. I'm getting the fuck out of this state, and this part of the country. I can't do the cold anymore."

Hannah was about to say something, but Stacy continued.

"I've been saving up to move to San Diego. I have a cousin out there who said I could stay with her until I can find my own place. Probably another month or two before I can get out of this hellhole. The sun, and the ocean, and the beaches, and hot guys on surf boards, hot guys in convertibles, hot guys with their shirts off, perfect weather year-round—and most importantly, no fucking snow."

Hannah nodded intently. Over the years, she'd had countless thoughts about running away from Colorado. Maybe a new setting would lessen the misery of Casey's murder, but eventually Hannah embraced that the weight of it would always be with her, no matter where she called home. No one could run from their nightmares. No one.

"I haven't told Bobby yet, but I don't think he'll care that much. I think he'd care more if someone broke in and stole his damn bong." Stacy held her empty cup with both hands. "Sorry for rambling. I'm just in a weird spot in my life."

"It's completely fine. I've been there before, and in some ways, I think I'm still in a weird spot." Hannah said.

Stacy forced a smile. "Well, what do you want to know about Julia?"

"What was your relationship to her?"

"She was my best friend. A girl I met in the fifth grade. We were in the same class and liked the same boy, and after he told us he liked another girl, we became friends. Then we went to middle school, high school, and college together. We were closer than most sisters. I think during our entire friendship, we probably didn't have more than a week that we didn't talk. She knew more about me than anyone."

The room grew quiet. Trying to fill the void, Hannah reached out and squeezed Stacy's hand.

"And I feel guilty for saying this, but when she was killed, my adolescence died. I became an adult that day, and I hate every minute of it," Stacy said, barely holding back tears.

"I feel the same way talking about my sister, and that was over a decade ago. I promise I wouldn't be here if I didn't think you could help the investigation."

"It's fine. I'll do whatever it takes to get this solved."

Hannah cleared her throat. "Do you know anyone who would want to hurt her?"

Stacy stared at the window for a moment. "I know it's cliché, but everyone loved her. She was the life of the party. She made everyone laugh. Made everyone feel special."

"And to your knowledge, was she seeing anyone?"

"For about the last two months or so, she was hanging out with this guy Ryan Kelly, but I wouldn't call it anything serious."

"Then what would you call it?"

"I'd say more of a friends-with-benefits situation."

"And who decided on that?"

"Julia. She wanted to get married and have kids, but Ryan wasn't the type of guy she could take home to her parents. They wanted her to marry a doctor or a lawyer or some shit, not some roughneck who works on an oil rig. I mean don't get me wrong, she liked Ryan, but didn't consider him boyfriend material, if you know what I'm saying. And to my understanding, Ryan was fine with their arrangement. I mean, what guy isn't?"

"Did you ever meet him?"

Stacy nodded. "Oh yeah, we all went to high school together. After that, me and Julia went to UW and he decided to get a job in the oil fields, but we stayed in touch throughout the years. He was one of the few guys we still talked to after graduation."

"Do you think he could've been involved in her murder?"

Stacy let out a brief chuckle. "Ryan? Hell no, he acts tough, but that guy is a softy. One night all three of us were watching *Titanic* and he started crying when Rose and Jack were in the water. We teased him for weeks about that." She paused for a second. "Anyways, he was up in Cody when everything happened, so there is no way he could've done it."

"Do you know if he was ever questioned by the police?"

"I don't, but probably not. I don't think anyone knew about their relationship except me, so the cops really didn't have a reason to talk to him. He didn't even know it happened until I was able to get a hold of him like two weeks later. He took it pretty hard."

"Did she ever mention anyone besides Ryan who might've been interested in her, or anyone who she might've been worried about?"

Stacy looked to the ceiling for a moment; the question seemed to weigh on her. Finally, she said, "Well, a couple weeks before everything happened, we were having lunch at McDonald's, and this older guy says hi to Julia, and—"

Hannah cut her off. "What did he look like?"

"Umm, I'd guess somewhere around forty, decent

looking for his age, a little beer belly and along grey beard."

Stacy stopped suddenly and looked directly at Hannah. Without saying a word, Hannah reached out and hugged her. They remained silent for almost a minute as Stacy cried on her shoulder. When they released the hug, Hannah's shirt was wet from the tears.

"I know this is extremely difficult, we can stop if you want," Hannah said.

"No, I'm fine. Keep asking your questions."

"Okay. What happened after the man said hi to Julia?"

Stacy took a deep breath. "Well, after Julia said bye to him, he stood there a moment, almost like he was waiting for her to say something else. Then he smiled and walked away without saying a word. It was really awkward. I asked her who it was, and she said just some customer from the bar. It was weird, but I really didn't think anything of it."

"Did you ever see him again?"

"Yeah, after we finished lunch, he was still in the parking lot, like three spots from ours. He glanced up, and waved, and Julia did like a half wave back."

"Was he in a Ford F-150?"

Slowly, Stacy nodded. "Yeah, black." With unsteadiness in her voice, she said, "Was that the man who killed her?"

Swallowing hard, Hannah felt her pulse begin to race. She was near certain the man who'd killed Casey and Julia was this same man Stacy had seen.

"I don't know."

"But you think it could be?"

"Possibly."

"Oh my god, I looked that fucker in the eyes and he smiled at me," Stacy said, her legs quivering.

In a reassuring voice, Hannah said, "I'm doing everything I can to find him."

Stacy slowly nodded.

"Have you talked to Ryan since that phone call about Julia's murder?"

Stacy looked at Hannah, then murmured, "Yeah, we talked after I moved up here like a couple times a week. In a weird way, I kinda felt like his therapist. Some nights I'd talk to him until two or three in the morning."

"Do you guys still talk?"

"It's been at least a month, maybe more. He got really busy with work, and I think we both got burnt out talking about Julia."

"Two questions. Is he still in Cody? And can I have his number?" Hannah said.

"Last time I talked to him he was, and yeah sure."

Stacy walked over to the desk and jotted down the number on a piece of paper, then ripped it out and handed it to Hannah.

Hannah studied the number until she memorized it.

"Good luck finding him, though. I think he moved out of the place he was living. He said he wanted to save money so he was going to start couch surfing, rent cheap motels and sleep in his car in the Wal-Mart parking lot. He works like eighty hours a week, so it really doesn't make sense to get an apartment."

"Would you happen to have a picture of him?"

A faint smile. "No, but Ryan is someone you can find on description alone. About six foot three, with bright red hair. I doubt there are a lot of ginger giants in Cody." She laughed. "And he has a tattoo on the inside of his forearm. Its two Chinese symbols. I think it means love and strength, or something like that."

They talked for a while longer, then after Hannah thanked Stacy, she got up and started to the door.

"Hannah," Stacy said, her eyes puffy. "Does this get easier?"

"Yeah, it does. Each day gets a little better," Hannah said, offering a half smile. That was a lie, but she didn't have the heart to tell Stacy that in ten years, she'd still miss Julia as much as she did the day she died.

The next morning, not wanting to call from the phone in her room, Hannah walked downstairs to the payphone and slipped two quarters into the coin slot and dialed the number Stacy had given her. Midway through the third ring, someone answered.

"Is Ryan there?" Hannah said.

"Nah, he moved out like three weeks ago," a man's voice answered, haggard and rough.

"Would you happen to know where I could find him?"

"I don't know where he's living, but when he's not working, he pretty much lives at the Silver Dollar Saloon, so I'm sure you could find him there."

Hannah thanked the man and hung up.

Three hours later, she arrived in Cody. It was a little after two in the afternoon, and she drove straight to the Silver Dollar Saloon. The parking lot was nearly empty, only two other cars. Exhausted from the drive, she decided to pull into an office park across the street and take a quick power nap.

When she awoke, it was almost five. The Silver Dollar Saloon parking lot was nearly full, and the sun was setting behind the bar. After rubbing the sleep out of her eyes, she hastily touched up her makeup and scampered across the street.

Inside the bar, a stale whiskey-and-cigarette stench filled the air, and the jukebox was playing "The Trooper" by Iron Maiden. There were about forty people, mostly males, scattered throughout the bar. About half of them were standing in a half circle at the bar top, drinking, laughing, and being rowdy. Near the middle was a tall man, towering above everyone else, with fire-engine-red hair.

Carefully, she walked to the bar, forcing her way through the group to the man, ignoring a hand that grabbed her butt. When she reached the man, she glanced at his forearm, and the Chinese symbol tattoos confirmed that it was indeed Ryan.

"Hey! Are you Ryan Kelly?" Hannah shouted over the music.

The man placed his hand on her shoulder and smiled, "I'm sorry sweetheart, but you're going to have to take a number," he said, laughing as he looked around at the other men in the group.

With her index finger, Hannah instructed him to lean into her. The man stared for a moment, then bent down.

Hannah inched toward the man, then whispered, "Want me to tell all your buddies that you cry like a baby at the end of *Titanic*?"

With a confused look, the man leaned back into the stool and inspected her from top to bottom. "Who the hell are you?" he said.

"I'm just a girl wondering if I could buy you a drink and ask you some questions."

"Questions? Questions about what?"

"Your relationship with Julia Boone."

He stared long and hard at Hannah, then said, "You've got ten minutes."

Hannah smirked and gestured to the bartender. "Could you get whatever he's drinking? And I'll take a whiskey and water."

"And a shot of Jameson," the man chimed in.

After they received the drinks, they sat at a table in the

back of the bar away from the rest of the patrons. The man did the shot and slammed the glass on the table, shaking the entire tabletop.

"Nothing like a shot of Jameson after a long day of work," the man said, licking his lips.

Hannah let her gaze linger on him. "I'm assuming you're Ryan Kelly from Laramie?"

"That is correct. And you are?"

"My name is Hannah Jacobs, and I'm investigating the murder of Julia Boone."

Ryan looked over his shoulder like he felt someone was standing behind him. "I had nothing to do with her murder, and I wasn't anywhere close to Laramie when it happened. I was on a job site three hundred miles away that day. And there are about twenty guys who could vouch for my whereabouts."

"Relax, I'm not here because I consider you a suspect. I just want to ask about you and Julia and the time leading up to the murder."

Behind Ryan there was a kid, maybe around six or seven, sitting in a booth by himself and drawing in a coloring book. Hannah became distracted by the child, and was about to say something to Ryan when a woman, presumably his mother, sat down next to him, holding a beer. She kissed the boy on the forehead, then picked up a crayon and started coloring with one hand, sipping on the beer with the other. Like she was keeping time, the woman slid out of the booth after a few minutes and returned to the bar, leaving the kid alone with a soda and the coloring book.

"I'm guessing you talked to Stacy," Ryan said, taking a drink. "Her and my brother were the only ones that knew about Julia and me, and there is no way in hell he'd tell you anything."

Hannah nodded, moving her glass in a slow twirl on the table.

His eyes were calming, mesmerizing. Hannah could see why Julia had a fleeting relationship with him. Hell, if she wasn't in the middle of a murder investigation, she might've been flirting with the intentions of going home with him and getting into another dysfunctional relationship.

"Tell me about you and Julia," Hannah said.

"Around February of this year, I was in between gigs and living back in Laramie, and we ran into each other at the grocery store and she asked if I wanted to hang out sometime. Two days later I was at her apartment and we were watching a movie, having some drinks, and the next thing I know I'm on her bed and our clothes are on the floor." Lifting the pint glass to his mouth, he drank deeply. "The sex was good and we had fun hanging out, but neither of us wanted anything serious. And for what it's worth, I feel like she was using me more than I was using her."

"And there was never discussion of it becoming more than a casual fling?"

"Nah, we both knew what it was. There were a few times when she was wasted that she said she wanted to be boyfriend girlfriend, but I chalked that up to drunk talk. I'm not going to lie and say I wasn't disappointed after the first time she said it."

"Did she ever mention anything about anyone following her?"

"No, but the last few times I was at her place it seemed like she was a little on edge. I asked if anything was going on, and she said she was fine. Then the night before I left to come up here, I stayed at her apartment, and after we had sex, I got the strangest feeling that someone was watching us through the blinds. I swear to God someone was. I jumped out of bed and ran to the window but nobody was outside."

Leaning back in her chair, Hannah let out a sharp sigh. Finally, she had the answer of why Julia was murdered at an unknown location instead of her apartment. Ryan staying overnight must've foiled the killer's plans, and abducting her on the trailhead that afternoon was his last opportunity for the murder before the waning crescent moon phase ended.

"And this was the night before she disappeared?"

"Yeah, like three in the morning. It spooked me so much that I couldn't go back to sleep. Finally at five I got up, showered real quick, then we said goodbye. I was on the road by five thirty, just as the sun was rising. That was the last time I ever saw her," Ryan said, his final words trailing off.

"Did you ever report any of this? The person watching you? Your relationship with Julia?"

"Yeah, I called the police station twice, and both times I left messages. Never heard back, so I assumed they either didn't deem my information important enough or they thought I was a liar." Ryan took the final sip from his glass, then rested it on the table. "When I got up here, I started working fourteen-hour days for the first two weeks, then I got the call from Stacy. I was fucking devastated." His eyes drifted to the ceiling, careful to avoid eye contact with Hannah. "As dumb as it sounds, I was starting to fall in love with her." He took a deep breath. "Well, I probably should get back to the guys."

Ryan stood up, pushed in the chair, and glanced down with desperate eyes. In a shallow voice, he said, "Please find whoever did this."

"I'm trying," Hannah said.

He tapped on the back of the chair and nodded, then turned and walked back to the group of men. Hannah watched them for several minutes, but Ryan never looked back.

She ran her index finger around the rim of the glass and thought about the drive back to Laramie. Almost four hundred miles of a dark and desolate two-lane highway. A long night of caffeine, cigarettes, and loud music. A long night alone.

SIX

Something woke Hannah. She sat up and turned to the curtains. Walking to the window with silent footsteps, she pulled them back just enough to see outside. Across the parking lot was what looked like a Ford F-150, idling its engine, smoke billowing out of the tailpipe. A streetlight shone onto the hood, and she could see hands on the steering wheel, but it was too dark to see the person inside.

For a long time, she remained still and watched the truck. It didn't move, and neither did the hands or person inside, almost like a mannequin. Occasionally, the engine revved before returning to the smooth idling.

It could be nothing, someone lost searching for a location on a map, or someone who'd decided to pull into the parking lot and take a nap instead of falling asleep on the highway. Or it could be him following her. Her gut told her it was him.

Bending down, she slipped on her shoes and glided across the carpet to the door. Doing the calculations, she knew she could be to the stairs in about twenty seconds, another fifteen to get down them, then about twenty seconds to cross the parking lot and be at the truck. Fifty-five seconds total. If he wasn't paying attention, she could be at the truck before he knew it. But then what?

The major details like what she'd do when she arrived at the truck didn't actually matter—all she knew was that she needed to get a glimpse of the man, or even better, the license plate. Warily, she placed her hand on the door handle and looked down at the carpet. At that moment, she would've traded anything to have her gun. Attempting to confront the man without a firearm was extremely foolish and could return the same outcome as what happened to Marshall in the parking garage. But she knew this might be her only opportunity to get this close to the man and the truck.

After taking a deep breath, she yanked the door open and instantly began sprinting across the walkway, passing a door every few seconds. At the stairway, she glanced back at the truck, and it was in the same position, still idling. She grabbed the railing and started leaping down the stairs, four at a time.

When her feet hit the pavement, she turned and started across the parking lot. Hannah was about halfway to the truck when the headlights turned on and it squealed out of the parking spot, heading directly toward her. The lights were blinding and the engine roared like a fighter jet.

For another few seconds, she continued sprinting, not fully grasping that the four-thousand-pound vehicle was mere seconds from hitting her. They were on a collision course, a one-sided game of chicken that Hannah would lose.

At about five feet, she lunged toward a parked car, and as she flew through the air, she shielded her face with her hands. Her right knee slammed into the fender, then her body crashed onto the hood of the car. The hard landing knocked the wind out of her, leaving her gasping for air. Seconds later she let out a scream and clutched her knee, bringing it toward her chest.

Lifting her head, she watched as the truck sped by at a blur. Through the black exhaust, she caught a glimpse of the bumper and license plate holder, but there was no license plate. It must've been removed or covered. For a fleeting moment, the brake lights flashed, and then the F-150 turned north onto Third Street. It was out of sight within seconds.

"Fuck, fuck," she screamed, realizing that she'd almost seen the face of the man who probably killed Casey, and there was a possibility she'd never get that close again.

She painstakingly pushed herself off the hood. First, the good leg touched the ground, and then she carefully applied weight onto the bad one, but it started to give out on her. Falling back into the car, she secured her hands on the hood while the bad leg hovered above the ground, limp.

Hannah rested against the car until she had the strength to make it back to the room, then staggered across the parking lot. As she climbed the stairs one by one, her knee throbbed as if someone was jamming a knife into it. It was unlike any pain she'd ever experienced.

In the room, she hobbled across the floor to her toiletry bag and removed a bottle of ibuprofen, swallowing two pills dry. One got caught in the back of her throat, and she had to choke it down. Then she went into the bathroom and slipped out of her clothes and turned the tap on hot. When the tub was half full, she eased herself into the water, drifting in and out of consciousness.

The following day, she rolled onto her stomach and looked at the clock radio. It was 2:13. Besides going to the bathroom twice, she remained in bed for thirty-six hours, and the TV was her only companion. A constant intake of pills kept her comatose, mostly masking the agony through sleep.

As the pain started to diminish, the bruise on her leg grew darker. A galaxy discoloration of blacks, blues, and purples. And even though she wasn't one for chalking something up to luck, mostly because she couldn't recall a time in her life that she'd ever been lucky, she was grateful that nothing was broken and the injury didn't require a hospital visit.

Hannah flung off the covers, then swung her legs out of bed and lowered them onto the carpet. With extreme caution, she stood on the left leg, then slowly added weight onto the right. The pain was present, but it was manageable, and she considered that a win.

She began pacing between the bathroom and the room door, using the wall, desk, and anything else within arm's reach as a support. Once she was confident the leg wouldn't give out on her, she grabbed the ice bucket and staggered to the ice machine at the end of the stairway. She filled up the bucket and returned to the room, then sat on the edge of the bed, and tied off the bag and rested it on her knee.

Then she grabbed her notebook and started flipping through pages until she located Tony's number. She picked up the headset and dialed. No answer. Hanging up, she waited two minutes and dialed again. Again, no answer.

Once almost every ice cube was melted, she went into the bathroom and dumped the water into the sink and washed her face. She took a long look at herself in the mirror. It'd been almost a week since she'd combed her hair, and three times as long since she'd washed it. She looked like shit, and she didn't care one bit.

She swallowed the last pill, then tossed on her backpack and left the room. Turning the doorknob, she checked that it was locked three times. She was only able to make it five steps before walking back and checking the door twice more.

As she drove to Walmart, seemingly every fourth vehicle was a black Ford F-150. Hannah knew she was experiencing frequency illusion, that phenomenon in which a person perceives something as being everywhere after becoming aware of it. Before the encounter in the motel parking lot, she'd suspected the killer drove a black F-150, but now she was certain that was his vehicle.

Inside the massive store, she navigated the aisles, keeping her head down and avoiding eye contact with everyone. After grabbing a bottle of ibuprofen and an elastic bandage wrap, she made her way to the checkout line. The cashier made small talk, but Hannah only nodded and thanked him as she took the receipt.

As she walked across the shopping center parking lot to the liquor store, her knee hurt with each step, but she endured the pain and forced herself to maintain a normal gait, making the limp virtually unnoticeable. If someone was watching her, she didn't want to appear vulnerable.

Back in the car, she pushed the driver's seat back, pulled up her jean leg, then tightly wrapped the bandage around her knee. There was throbbing for about thirty seconds, and then it gradually diminished. Leaning down, she lowered the jean leg, then took two quick sips of whiskey. She returned the bottle to the bag, lit a cigarette, and started the car.

As Hannah turned into Tony's apartment complex, she saw four police cars and an ambulance, all with their sirens off. A group of police officers and first responders hovered around Tony's apartment, and yellow crime scene tape crisscrossed the front door, extending out into the parking spaces in front of the building. Her heart sank—*was he dead?*

Parking diagonally over two spots, she jammed the car into park and then jumped out. As she rushed to Tony's apartment, an officer glanced over and saw her. He ducked under the tape and stopped her before she could reach the crime scene perimeter.

"I'm sorry, ma'am, you can't go in there—it's an active investigation," the officer said, holding one hand up.

"Where is Tony?" Hannah said.

"I'm not at liberty to say."

"Is he dead?"

"I can't discuss the whereabouts of the occupants of the residence."

"Is Sheriff Harris here?" she asked, louder this time.

"Ma'am, you're going to have to step back or I'm going to have to arrest you and issue an obstruction of justice citation."

From the inside of the apartment, Rick peered out. "Hannah?"

Sidestepping the officer, she yelled, "Can you please tell me what the hell is going on?"

The sheriff stepped out of the doorway and strode toward Hannah, stroking his mustache as if he was trying to conceal his mouth.

"Come on, let's get away from all of this," Rick said, grabbing her forearm.

"I need to know if he's dead," she said very quietly.

Rick didn't say a word, and they walked in silence until they reached the end of the building. Hannah placed her hand on the wall, her legs trembling. Rick took a while, observing the officers congregating around Tony's apartment, and then he quietly slipped around the corner.

Leaning against the siding, he took off his cowboy hat and ran his fingers through his thinning hair, then removed a pack of cigarettes from his front pocket and offered Hannah one. She declined the offer with a silent gesture.

Glancing up to the ashen sky, she said again, "Is he dead?"

After a long silence, Rick said, "I'm so sorry."

"What happened?"

"I don't want to say until I get word from the medical examiner."

"Please, I need to know what happened."

"This doesn't go beyond this conversation," he said, taking a drag.

Hannah nodded.

"I swear if I find out you talk to anyone, or if it leaks to the press, I'll throw you in jail so fast your head will spin."

"Tony was the only person I knew in this fucking town, and I can promise you I won't talk to anyone at that bush league newspaper, so you have nothing to worry about."

He peered around the corner again, then back at her. "Officially, we'll have to wait on the toxicology report to get the cause of death, but unofficially, I'm fairly certain it was an overdose. There were two empty OxyContin bottles on the nightstand and a half bottle of vodka in the kitchen."

Prescription pills scared Hannah, and as much as she wanted relief from her anxiety, she knew she couldn't take them. In her late teens, she'd been prescribed Prozac, and everything was fine for a little over a month, but she was forced to stop after she began fantasizing about running across her living room and jumping out the second-story window.

"And you don't suspect foul play?" Hannah said.

Rick looked down at her and shook his head. "No,

there is no sign of a struggle, and no sign of forced entry. Nothing to indicate that this was more than an accidental overdose."

"I'm almost certain he didn't take pills."

Rick took a deep drag and stared into the field behind the apartment complex. "Oxy has been killing people on each coast for the last few years or so, and now it's starting to penetrate to the middle of the country. First New York and Los Angeles, then sooner or later everything makes its way to Denver and then Laramie." He sighed. "That stuff is as deadly as it comes—take a couple pills and drink some beers, then pass out and you'll never wake up."

"I've known pill poppers, and he didn't have the mannerisms of one. He was a pothead, and liked getting drunk, but that's it."

"I know you don't believe me, but it's pretty apparent that it was an overdose," he said, placing his hand on her shoulder. "I'm truly sorry, Hannah."

After a moment, he removed his hand and started back down the sidewalk. Hannah watched as he ducked under the police tape and slipped back into the apartment and out of sight. Using her sleeve, she wiped her eyes, then started across the parking lot to her car.

In her periphery, she spied Deputy Earl talking to two other officers next to the ambulance. They made eye contact with each other, and neither of them wanted to break away. Then he winked and turned back to the other officers.

When she was about ten feet away, Earl said with a smirk, "At least we have one less fag in town."

Hannah froze, and a fury churned within her like no other she'd ever experienced before. She wanted to claw out his eyes and kick out his teeth, then rip out his Adam's apple and shove it down his throat.

Instantly she launched herself toward Earl with her fists clinched, arms cocked, ready to punch him square in the face, hoping to get at least two punches before anyone could react.

"Fuck you, you piece of shit! Fuck you!"

As she was about to strike the deputy, one of the other officers turned around. Almost in slow motion, he took one step toward her and brought his arms down, palms open, and shoved Hannah in the shoulder, completely altering her trajectory.

For a second, as Hannah fell through the air, she was weightless and at peace, but she knew that would end once she landed. Falling sideways, she shielded her face with her right arm and prepared to break the fall with her left. When she slammed onto the ground, the movie-style slow motion ended and her left palm slid across the pavement. The rest of her body followed.

Looking up from the ground, she saw Earl hovering over her, gun drawn. From the look in his eyes, she knew he wanted to kill her.

"Make another move and I'll blow your fucking head off," he said.

Hannah was motionless, her palms planted squarely on the ground.

"I dare you to move an inch, you little bitch."

"Earl! Put your weapon away! Now!" Rick yelled from across the parking lot.

Hannah could see the sheriff running toward them. Then her eyes turned back to the gun and Earl's steady finger on the trigger.

"Earl! I said put your weapon away!"

"Next time you won't be this lucky," Earl said through clinched teeth.

Earl stepped back and holstered the weapon. Moments

later, Rick grabbed him and started forcing him in the opposite direction.

"Will you guys put him in the back of my car and make sure you confiscate and clear his firearm," Rick said to the half dozen police officers who'd congregated in a half circle around Hannah.

As an officer ushered Earl away, Rick rushed over to Hannah and knelt in front of her.

"Are you okay?" he said.

All Hannah wanted to do was break down and cry, but she wasn't about to fall apart in front of half of the Laramie police force—not Rick, and especially not Earl.

"What are you going to do about that fucking lunatic?" Hannah shouted, pointing at Earl.

"I will discipline him later, but for now, are you okay? Do you need medical assistance?"

"No, I'm fine, I'm fine," Hannah said.

"Here, let me help you up," Rick said, extending his hand.

Hannah scrutinized it for a bit, half expecting he'd pull it away at the last moment and she'd drop like a stone back to the pavement. Finally, she reached for him, and he helped her to her feet. While she was brushing off her pants, she noticed the half dozen road rash cuts on her palm and the rip in the back of her jeans.

Rick said something, but Hannah didn't hear him. "What was that?" she muttered.

"Do you want to press charges?" he said.

Hannah stopped brushing her jeans and peered up at him. "Will it get that asshole fired?"

He hesitated for a second, keeping his lips tight, then evenly shook his head.

"Then what the fuck is the point?"

"Well, it would go into his record, and if he gets enough

formal complaints, disciplinary action will be taken.”

Hannah covered her mouth and rolled her tired eyes, not needing to say a word about what she thought of the situation.

After a large inhale through her nose, she spoke. “Can you at least try to keep that asshole away from me? I’ve caught him following me at least once, and I’m positive it’s been more than that, and when I did catch him, he wasn’t even trying to conceal that he was following me.”

She waited a moment for a response, but there wasn’t one. Rick stared blankly at her, trying to say something reassuring.

“Pathetic,” she said, turning away and starting to her car.

Rick followed her. “This is nothing against you.”

Stopping on a dime, Hannah turned around. “Well, he has a funny way of fucking showing it,” she snarked.

“He takes his job very seriously and is very protective of the town and its residents and very suspicious of outsiders.”

“I’d hate to see how he treats real criminals.”

By the time she reached her car, there was a sharp pain in her lower back, and by the time she arrived back at the motel, her tail bone was throbbing. Hannah knew that she’d be sore for a few days and the bruise would persist for at least a week. The tailbone combined with the knee made walking a chore, and she felt like a seventy-year-old woman after knee surgery and a hip replacement.

She curled up under the covers and buried her head into her arms, shielding her eyes from the world. Casey’s murder had tormented her nearly every day for the past ten years, yet the closer she got to solving the case, the more she second-guessed herself, as if she were searching in the wrong direction.

What if the leads turned into dead end, after dead end, after dead end? What if the man in the truck wasn't the murderer? And what if Tony didn't die of an overdose? What if he was murdered because Hannah had started investigating the string of unsolved murders? And what if the ex-sheriff was right, that it was a University of Wyoming student who'd graduated and moved away and never returned? If that was the case, it'd never get solved. And what if the planned two weeks in Laramie turned into a month, then two months? At some point, she'd have to return home, case solved or not.

As the ceiling fan rotated, she became spellbound by the sound. She envisioned what Casey would be doing if she were still alive. Her sister would probably be married with a couple of kids. Casey had always wanted to be a mother, and Hannah had always wanted to be an aunt. That'd never happen. Never.

The thoughts spinning in her head became overwhelming, and she felt like the weight of everything was about to crash down onto her. When Hannah found herself in this state, she envied Casey. That she was dead, and at peace, and no longer had to live this life. Hannah hated herself for thinking that.

Rolling onto her back, she lay motionless, mentally paralyzed, staring blankly at the ceiling. All she wanted was to sleep, but her mind was racing and wasn't about to stop.

Then the mental filter that blocked all of her heinous thoughts stopped working. The flood gates were open, and they couldn't be turned off, and the urge to cut became overwhelming and uncontrollable.

Hannah sprang out of bed, frantic, and began searching the room for something sharp enough to penetrate her flesh. To her dismay, there wasn't a knife, or a razor blade, or any other of her habitual go-to objects, and she began cursing herself for not bringing a blade.

"Fuck," she said in a long, drawn-out sigh.

Maybe the front desk had a supply of disposable razors for travelers, or maybe there was a vending machine that contained toiletries. Highly doubtful. She could break an empty whiskey bottle against the bathroom counter and use the broken glass as a cutting device. But that would result in hundreds of glass shards that'd get embedded into the carpet and tile and could possibly cut future guests in the room. Hannah didn't want to injure anyone besides herself.

She thought back to one of her weakest moments, when she'd attempted to use a butter knife. The blade was dull and wouldn't penetrate her skin, so she used a lighter and held the flame under the metal until it was red hot, then pressed it firmly against her bicep. The skin bubbled around the edges of the knife, and she blacked out from the pain. The burn took almost four months to heal completely. After that, she promised to never burn herself again.

Standing in the middle of the room, she felt a cold shiver course through her body. After wiping her face and rubbing her eyes, she glanced down at the case notes next to the bed. Dropping to her knees, she feverishly began rummaging through the stack of paper on the floor until she found the picture of Casey. Hannah grabbed the picture and crawled into bed, holding it tight against her chest, heavy tears rolling down her face.

Sometime after dusk, a knock came at the door. A little knock, like the person on the other side didn't want anyone else to hear.

Hannah pulled her head out of the sheets and peered at the door. She had no idea who it could be. It was too late for housekeeping, and if the front desk needed anything, they would've called. It could've been Mark, the man from room 221, the one she'd had a disjointed conversation with a few nights ago. Doubtful—she'd been awkward and had most likely scared him away. Maybe it was Rick or one of his goons from the police department coming to arrest her for attempted assault on an officer, and if that was the case, she'd throw punches until the handcuffs were around her wrists. Or maybe it was Earl, coming to finish what he'd wanted to do earlier in the day, but he probably would've just kicked the door in and started firing without saying a word.

Hannah slid off the bed and tiptoed across the carpet in her bare feet. At the door, she looked through the peephole, but there was nothing. Dead quiet. Seconds later, three more knocks vibrated against her forehead.

"Hannah, are you there?" a voice said, timid.

Even though Hannah knew the swing bar lock was secured, she checked the latch, pushing it tight. Carefully, she stepped away from the door, a precaution in case whoever was on the other side decided to kick it open when they heard her voice.

"Who's there?" she shouted in a rough, menacing tone.

There was a brief hesitation, then after a cough, a voice said, "You don't know me, but my name is Nicholas. I'm Tony's friend."

Hannah immediately opened the door and gestured him inside. "Come in," she said.

They sat on the bed facing the blank TV screen. She offered him a water or a warm Coke, but he declined. So, she grabbed the bottle of Jack and extended it to him instead. Without hesitation, he accepted the bottle, spun off the lid, and took a long swig.

"Thanks," he said, coughing hard, eyes watering.

He offered the bottle back to Hannah, and she took a quick pull before placing it back on the nightstand.

"I'm so sorry about Tony. I barely knew him, but he seemed like an amazing person."

"He was," Nicholas said, holding back the tears. "Tony was one of a kind. You either loved him or hated him, and I definitely loved him." He paused for a moment. "I'm really going to miss him.

The room fell silent. After a few seconds, Nicholas unzipped a backpack and removed a thick stack of paper.

"A couple of nights ago, I was over at Tony's place, and he asked me for a favor."

When Hannah had first heard Nicholas's voice, she wasn't sure why he was at her motel room, but as she watched him remove the stack, she became almost ecstatic, having a hunch about what he was about to give her.

"Under normal circumstances, I would never do this, but I'm leaving Wyoming. It's not safe for people like me here," he said, looking at Hannah.

"I understand." She held his gaze.

The look in his eyes projected sadness. It was an expression Hannah had seen countless times in the mirror.

"This should be what you're looking for. The names, addresses, phone numbers, birthdays and every other piece of personal information you'd need of everyone who's registered a Ford F-150 in Albany, Carbon, Platte, and Laramie counties."

He offered the papers to Hannah, and she grabbed them. Already, she'd started doing the math in her head. Fifteen entries per page, about twenty pages.

"There has to be at least a few hundred names," Hannah muttered while leafing the pages.

In a tired voice, he said, "Four hundred and fifty-six, to be exact."

"Fuck, I knew it was going to be a lot, but I didn't think it would be that many."

"Men in Wyoming love their big trucks, and from my experience, a lot of them are making up for something else that is lacking."

Hannah stopped skimming the pages and looked over at Nicholas with a smile.

"Sorry, it's true," he said, shrugging.

They both laughed.

As he was about to get up, Hannah asked the question she wanted to ask the moment he walked into her room. "What do you think happened to Tony?"

His eyes drifted to the ceiling, as if trying to avoid the question. After a long pause, he said, "I don't believe a word those fucking cops are saying. In the six months we hung out, I never once saw him pop any pills. Nothing. That wasn't his thing. Yeah, he loved getting fucked up, but not with pills. Something doesn't add up. The last time I saw him, he was his normal self. There was no way he was taking Oxy or whatever the cops are saying." He shook his head and continued. "If I had to bet, I'd say those cops had a hand in it. Some of those guys are crooked as a dog's hind leg."

"Like Earl?" Hannah said.

"Yeah, especially that cocksucker. I hate him with a passion."

"You and me both."

Nicholas broke into a smile, then glanced down at his watch. "Well, I probably should get going. I want to be as far from here as possible by midnight."

"Where are you going?"

"I'm not sure yet. I have some family down in Texas,

so maybe there. Maybe Arizona. I really don't know." He took an extended breath. "The funeral is in Chicago on Wednesday, and I really want to go, but it's probably best I don't. His family didn't know about him, and about our relationship. And they're very religious, Catholic or something. They won't understand. I think I'll just celebrate his life the way he'd want me too. A few shots, smoke a joint, and spend the night listening to Led Zeppelin in my headphones as loud as humanly possible."

Once Nicholas was gone, Hannah latched the chain and jumped onto the bed. Reaching across, she pulled the stack of papers toward her, then flicked through the pages, creating a slight fan effect. She was confident that Casey's killer would be one of the 456. For a minute or two, she stared at the top page, then after a long sigh, she picked up a Sharpie and began crossing off names.

The first eliminations were females. Hannah was certain he wasn't married, and on the off-chance that he was, he wouldn't allow a woman to register his truck in her name. He hated women, and probably treated them worse than his dog.

The next round of eliminations were anyone born after 1973. Hannah decided on that year because anyone would've only been fifteen when Casey was murdered and would not have been able to obtain a driver's license. It did occur to her that in Wyoming, especially in rural areas of the state, kids started driving at twelve or fourteen, but she was confident that someone that young couldn't have committed Casey's brutal murder. Casey was petite, but she was a fighter, and a younger teenager couldn't have overpowered her.

The next eliminations were F-150s that were manufactured after 1989. This elimination worried her, because the killer could've traded in and purchased a newer truck after Casey's murder, but most people in this region tended to do their own repairs and would drive a vehicle until the wheels fell off. Hannah was banking that he was mechanically inclined, the kind too stubborn to purchase a new vehicle.

The next elimination was easy—cross off any entries with an apartment number in the address. Odds were that Julia had been murdered at the killer's residence, and it would be almost impossible to carry her in and out, then rape and torture her for hours before killing her without anyone seeing or hearing anything.

About an hour later, the list was narrowed down to five possible suspects. Hannah rewrote each of the five names along with the corresponding details into her notepad. She watched as the ink dried, blowing on it to speed up the process, then stared at the page for a long time, fixating on every name.

SEVEN

U nsure of the actual name of the bar, Hannah along with most patrons referred to the establishment as "Bar Bar," a callout to the double-sided sign that hung above the front door that simply read "Bar." Some establishments didn't need an official name, and this was one of them.

It was a few blocks away from the Colorado State University campus in Fort Collins, but students avoided it like the plague, only mistakenly wandering in to use the bathroom or as a test of masculinity for frat boys who after five minutes retreated faster than a hiker stumbling across a momma bear and her cubs.

The clientele was rough, but that didn't concern Hannah—she'd been in seedier places in worse parts of Denver. In fact, she preferred business meetings at dive bars, because for the most part, conducting illegal activity never raised suspicion with the drunks and the staff.

Staring out the window, past the neon Pabst Blue Ribbon sign, she watched the setting sun and tried not to think about the dull ache in her stomach. With every foreign feeling, she always presumed the worst. A blood clot, cancer, a stroke. Something that'd kill her. Death was constantly on her mind, and the more idle her thoughts were, the stronger the thoughts of death. It was as if her mind was always fighting against her.

She was about to ask the bartender if there was something to read, a newspaper, a penny saver, anything to preoccupy her thoughts, when Doug entered

the bar. Hannah gestured him to the booth and sat back down. They greeted each other, and then Hannah slid a drink across the table.

"I see that it's nice and watered down," Doug said.

Glancing at her watch, Hannah said, "Well, if you'd been on time, it wouldn't be."

"Traffic sucked. Two years ago, I used to be able to do this drive in forty-five minutes. It just took me almost an hour and fifteen. Damn everyone for moving here."

"The secret is out about Colorado. You can't stop the migration now."

"I wish I could. I fucking hate all these Cali people moving into my neighborhood."

"They're not so bad," Hannah said.

"Yeah, neither is a root canal," Doug said, then slammed about half the drink in one large gulp.

Hannah let out a small chuckle. No matter her mood, Doug always brought a smile to her face.

"This was the best I could do on short notice," Doug said, sliding a brown paper bag across the table.

Hannah felt a flash of worry, but then she remembered that this bar was a place where some patrons came to score a bag of coke or get a bathroom blow job for a discount, so the two of them doing a small arms deal shouldn't raise any suspicions.

"The serial numbers have been scratched off, so if you get caught with it, you don't know me."

Hannah looked down at him and raised her eyebrows. "You know who you're talking to right? Have I ever done you wrong?"

"I know you wouldn't, but it's operating procedure and just something I say to everyone." He cocked his head. "Are you in some kind of trouble?"

"With this little guy I think I'll be fine," Hannah said, tapping on the bag. "What do I owe you?"

"For you, $100. That's the friends and family discount."

Doug finished the drink, set the glass on the table, and gestured to the bartender to bring another round.

Hannah slid six twenties across to him. "Thanks, and there's a little extra for your time."

Without looking at the money, Doug grabbed it and stuffed it into his pants pocket.

"Angie has been asking when you're going to come over. I've been making up excuses, but I don't think it's going to work for much longer. Pretty soon she's going to make me kidnap you and bring you to the house."

Angie was Doug's wife. They'd been high school sweethearts, and even though she was only seven years older than Hannah, Hannah thought of Angie like an aunt. As pathetic as it was, she was Hannah's closest female friend.

"Once I'm back in Denver, I promise I'll come over with a bottle of tequila, and I won't let her pass out until it's finished."

"I'm holding you to that."

The bartender dropped off two drinks, and Hannah provided Doug some details about her time in Laramie, the sheriff, breaking into the retirement home, traveling to Billings and Cody, and how she felt she was getting closer to finding a suspect.

She deliberately left out the parts about someone possibly cutting her fuel line and someone being parked outside of her motel room, and that she'd narrowed it down to five suspects and was about to visit each of their residences, which was why she required the gun. When Doug asked why she needed it, she told him it was for her protection because she suspected someone was following her.

"The guy is mostly harmless. I just want to use this to scare him off if he comes knocking on my door," Hannah said.

Sometimes a lie is the best option. There was no point in making him worry, and she knew if she told him the truth, he would insist on going to Laramie with her, and there was no reason to put him in harm's way.

Twenty minutes and two tequila shots later, they hugged and said their goodbyes, then headed in opposite directions on the sidewalk.

As Hannah was about to cross the street to the lot where she'd parked, she stopped on the corner next to a streetlight. The base of the pole was corroded with rust—years, maybe decades of winter road salt treatment that had deteriorated the once-pristine metal, making gaps large enough to fit her fist. A strong wind could probably snap it in two, dropping it like an evergreen.

Across the street, in the parking spot next to her car, there was a windowless Econoline van parked facing the opposite direction. The sliding door was parallel with her driver's side, with about three feet separating the two. The parking lot wasn't even half full, and the van hadn't been there when Hannah parked. If possible, she always parked a few spots away from the nearest vehicle. There were at least thirty open spots, and there was no valid reason why the van should've been parked there—unless they were waiting for her.

Glancing to her left, Hannah pressed the crosswalk button three times, then turned and studied the van. It had Colorado license plates. In a whisper, she repeated the number until she memorized it. The back windows were either covered with black curtains or had an illegal shade of tint. If it was tint, and they were using binoculars, she'd most likely been made, but if they were curtains, the chances that the occupant had seen her yet were slim.

Across the street, on the back side of the parking lot, was a three-story parking garage. From the top level, she'd have a direct line of sight to inside the cabin of the van.

Hannah pressed the crosswalk button three more times, and seconds later the signal turned white. Casually, Hannah strolled across the street to the parking garage, then pulled the stairway door open and started sprinting up the stairs, three at a time. The stairwell was dark and reeked of urine, and Hannah almost tripped on a homeless person passed out about halfway between the second and third stories.

On the top level, Hannah bent over, placed her hands on her knees, and gasped for air. It was situations like this that made her realize how out of shape she was, and how much she needed a gym membership.

Creeping across the cement, Hannah made it to the perimeter. She inched up and peered over the edge and down into the van. It was at least three hundred yards away, but she was able to see inside the cabin. There were no signs of anyone. No movement. Nothing.

Anxiously, she glanced down to the sidewalk—about a thirty-foot drop. Heights were something Hannah avoided. Every time she stood at the edge of a cliff, or on a balcony, or almost anything that was more than three stories tall, she fantasized about the fall. As a teenager, she'd visited

Flaming Gorge dam in Utah, and from the crest of the dam peered down five hundred feet to the raging waters below, her palms turning sweaty and her throat going dry. The longer she gazed into the abyss, the greater the urge became to climb onto the ledge and step off. It was the Call of the Void, the compulsion to jump. It wasn't that she actually wanted to plunge to her death, it was her intrusive thoughts raging out of control.

After five minutes, Hannah decided the driver of the van was probably just an asshole who didn't respect personal space, and it was safe to return to her car.

When she exited the parking garage stairwell, the van was still in the same spot, and she watched for another minute. Pulling her keychain out of her pocket, she readied the car key, then carefully started across the lot. The closer she got, the faster she walked.

As Hannah approached her car, she veered to the passenger side. She unlocked the door, jumped inside and pushed down on the door lock button about a dozen times. Climbing over the center console, she jammed the key into the ignition and squealed out of the parking spot. In the rearview mirror, she kept one eye on the van, but there was no movement.

Back in Laramie, Hannah drove straight to Walmart and purchased two boxes of ammunition, then drove ten blocks away to an empty parking lot. Pulling on the seat lever, she pushed the seat back as far as it'd go, then picked up the Beretta and held it for a few minutes, familiarizing herself with the contour. The firearm was smaller, lighter than her gun. At first it felt foreign, but the longer she held it, the more at ease she became that it'd suffice. And even though she had no intention of pulling the trigger, she knew there might not be another option.

For a moment, she thought about driving farther out of town and taking target practice, but if someone called the police, and she was arrested with a gun without a serial number, she'd be facing weeks, maybe months of jail time. Instead, she secured the gun in her purse, then leaned back into the seat.

In a field across the street, a group of kids no older than twelve were playing football. In ten minutes, there was three touchdowns, two interceptions, and at least a dozen non-called passing interference penalties. Either they didn't know the rules or they didn't care.

Reaching down, Hannah grabbed her notepad and propped it onto the steering wheel, then stared at the five names on the page. In a steady rhythm, she drummed with her thumb on the bottom of the pad, hoping a name would jump out to her. But none of them did. The longer she examined each name, the less certain she became that one of them was the killer, and as her vision went out of focus, they all started to blend into one.

She lit a cigarette then continued to flick the red lighter. Flame on, flame off, flame on, flame off, over and over and over again. When she finished the cigarette, she stabbed it in the ashtray then placed the lighter on the passenger seat. With her eyes closed, she slid her finger up and down across the notepad, then after about twenty seconds, she stopped and slowly opened her left eye.

"Well, Richard Harrison, I guess you're going to get an unexpected visitor tonight."

Reaching into the backseat, she grabbed a Wyoming road atlas and located Richard's address in the index, then turned to the corresponding page. On the map, it was about three inches away, and according to the scale, that was about twelve miles. Probably five as the crow flies. Less than a twenty-minute drive, and probably less than thirty minutes before she was on his property. She lit another cigarette and tried not to think about the worst-case scenarios.

About three miles outside of Laramie, train crossing gates lowered, and she steadily slowed the car until it came to a stop in front of the tracks. For about a minute, there was nothing except the flashing orange lights on the gate, and she briefly considered circumventing them, but then the squeal of the train shattered the silence. The single light of the locomotive appeared on the tracks, and the ground shook as the freight train traveled, seemingly stretching for miles. Several minutes later the caboose passed and the crossing gates rose, and once again the night was silent, almost like the massive machine had never been there.

Shortly after the train tracks, the pavement gave way to gravel and there was nothing but open land, bales of hay and trees. Not a single man-made structure in sight, and the nearest house could've been a mile, if not more. With the sun setting to the west, it was quite serene.

Rural towns like Laramie tended to have a centralized population within the city limits, but miles outside of town, past Main Street and highways and interstates, the land would become very remote and desolate. Even though Richard only lived twelve miles from her motel, it felt like it could've been a hundred.

As Hannah approached Richard's house, she rolled slow past the driveway. The house was about fifty feet back, down a single-lane dirt road surrounded by trees.

The lights were on inside the house. No one was visible, and there were no vehicles parked on the property, but there was an oversized detached garage toward the back.

She continued on the road for almost another mile until she came to a pullout with a decrepit shed. Hannah buried the car behind it, then turned off the headlights and sat for a bit, waiting for dusk to turn into night.

"Sabotage" by Beastie Boys was playing at a low volume, low enough that Hannah's humming almost drowned out the stereo. When the song was over, she turned off the car, slipped the key into her jeans pocket, and opened the door. The dome light turned on and Hannah glanced up at it, staring for a moment. Then she reached up and pried off the covering to the light, unscrewed the bulb, and placed it on the passenger seat. No need to bring unwanted attention if someone followed her back from the house.

As she stepped out, the cold air took her breath. The temperature must've fallen at least twenty degrees since she'd left Laramie. After zipping up her coat, she checked the load in the gun for the fifth time, then secured it in her belt and started back down the road.

About a half mile into the walk, headlights appeared on the horizon. Hannah turned back and briefly considered running to her car, but the distance was too great, and there was no way she'd reach it before the oncoming vehicle. If she stayed on the shoulder, though, she'd be an easy target. With no other viable options, Hannah jumped into the brush and knelt on a weathered log, holding the gun against her chest, preparing herself for a possible shootout.

All she could think about was that Richard knew the color, make, and model of her car, and if he would've been looking out a window, he most likely would've recognized her cruising by like she was rolling through a

California stop. She considered herself a very skilled PI, but sometimes she still made rookie mistakes, and this was one of those.

Under her breath, she started cursing herself with self-deprecation, then muttered, "Please be someone else. Please keep driving. Don't stop. I don't want to shoot anyone tonight."

The engine grew louder and louder, the lights brighter and brighter. After taking a small step forward, Hannah slid her finger onto the trigger and waited.

Moments later, the car sped by, and the sounds of teenagers laughing broke through the roar of the engine. As soon as the car passed, the smell of exhaust and marijuana hung in the air. Hannah turned and watched the car disappear into a cloud of dust.

She rubbed her eyes and let out a long sigh. She had to be very careful—if that car had stopped, her paranoia could've resulted in shooting kids on a joy ride getting high. Sometimes her anxiety doubled as paranoia.

Once she was confident the car wasn't returning, she stood up, brushed herself off, then continued down the road.

About a hundred feet before the driveway, Hannah carefully cut through the dense woods and underbrush, trudging cautiously, finally stopping at a tree that provided both concealment and a direct line of sight of the house. Everything looked exactly the same as when Hannah had driven by forty minutes ago. She listened to the night. Nothing but the constant buzz from somewhere, probably electricity lines cutting through the forest. The landscape looked familiar, but she wasn't certain what it reminded her of. Maybe she'd seen something like it in a magazine. Or maybe on a TV show, or in a movie. Or maybe it was remnants of a dream.

From her vantage point, she could see inside three first-floor windows of the house. A view of almost the entire living room, as well as the kitchen and dining room. *Jeopardy* was playing on the TV, and the lights in the kitchen were on. The house was neglected, and if not for the lights and the TV being on, she would've assumed it was deserted.

Hannah turned her gaze onto the garage. It was large, very large, and probably could hold at least four vehicles. It was about thirty feet off the side of the house, and twenty feet away from the forest, and Hannah was certain that as long as someone wasn't watching out the kitchen window, she could sprint from the trees to the garage door without being detected.

Still apprehensive, she watched the house for a long time, long enough to see Jeopardy end, and the next show, a hospital-based drama start and make its way through two commercial breaks. Nothing inside the house moved. And even though she was carrying a gun, she wanted to be certain that the house was empty, or if someone was home, that they were fast asleep or passed out. She didn't want to get trapped in the garage with only one known possible route for escape.

Ten minutes later, she decided it was time, and silently made her way along the tree line until she was directly across from the garage door. Turning to the house, she could see through the patio door into the kitchen. There was no one in sight. For a long moment, she stood still, listening, but there was nothing. Then she took a deep breath and darted across the open field.

When she approached the garage, the door was ajar about an inch. She placed her palm on it and pushed it open just wide enough for her to squeeze through. Hannah stepped inside, then closed it with the same methodical precision she'd used to open it. A sweet smell in the air, probably antifreeze.

Hannah waited until she was certain no one saw her, then removed a flashlight from her jacket and turned it on. Parked on the opposite side of the garage was the only vehicle—a black Ford F-150. For a few seconds, she admired the truck and her find, nearly forgetting that a potential serial killer could be thirty feet away.

Stealthily, she moved across the cement to the truck. Studying the vehicle, she was 90 percent certain it was the same truck from the Motel 6 parking lot. The same sun-faded paint, the same tint on the windows, the same bumper and headlights. There was a torn University of Wyoming Cowboys sticker on the bumper that she didn't remember, but in the chaos of the truck attempting to run her over, it might've been a detail she'd overlooked.

Crouching down, she scurried across the cement to the driver's side, then stood slowly to inspect the cab. Clean. Not a piece of trash in sight, no gas station cups, no candy bar wrappers, and no cigarette butts. It looked like someone cleaned it routinely.

She placed her fingers on the handle and pulled the door open. The hinge gave a distinct creak despite her slowness and caution, and she instantly turned back to the garage door. She watched it for a minute, expecting someone to barge through the door. Nobody.

Turning back to the truck, she stretched out across the bench seat and opened the glovebox. Then she removed everything from inside and dropped it on the floorboard. With one hand on the flashlight, she used her free hand to flip through the contents. The third document was a vehicle registration, registered to Richard Harrison. Delicately, she folded it up and slipped it into her front pocket, then stuffed all the other documents back into the glovebox.

Just as she was about to start searching the bed of the truck, a voice echoed. "Who the hell is in my garage?"

Hannah turned to the door, leaning hard into the truck while reaching for the gun in her belt. Her breathing was heavy. She started inching toward the door, trying to get a view of the patio and the voice.

"I know someone is out there. I hear you rustling around," the man yelled, louder now.

Hannah remained still, not wanting to confirm her presence.

"If that's you, Eddie, you better not be stealing anything," the man said. "And I think you've already taken everything of value anyways."

As she made her way to the door, she could hear him shuffling around on the patio. His movements were loud and deliberate.

"Eddie, if that's you, say something," the man said with a touch of fear.

At the door, Hannah peered through the crack. Standing on the patio was a man leaning on a cane. The dull porch light behind him created a silhouette effect.

"So, you don't want to identify yourself? Robbing a blind man, you damn coward!"

She froze. *A blind man?* She thought for a moment. Could he be lying? Could this be one of his many ruses to obtain the upper hand on his victims?

Hannah studied the man for a long moment, and as her eyes adjusted to the light, his features became clearer. He was frail and seemed nervous, wearing oversized black sunglasses covering half his face, and leaning on a cane like he'd tumble over if it weren't there. He looked more like Wilford Brimley than Ted Bundy. Either he really was blind, or he was putting on an Oscar-worthy performance.

"You have about ten seconds to identify yourself or I'm calling the damn cops."

"Don't call the police! I'm a private investigator, and I'm searching for a Ford F-150 that's been involved in a series of unsolved crimes," Hannah shouted across the yard.

During the long silence that followed, Hannah began second-guessing herself. In situations like these, it was always better to tell a lie first, then the truth later if needed.

After about twenty seconds, he said, "Come on out of the garage and talk to me."

Hannah contemplated the request. Her first thought was that she could sprint out, then run the mile to her car. The problem with that scenario was that she hadn't run for any distance, let alone a mile, in years, probably not since high school gym class. And if there was someone else in the house, they'd easily track her down in a car. Another option would be to hightail it into the forest and make her way to the car from the woods. Luckily, Hannah had a keen sense of direction and could always identify north, so getting lost didn't worry her—it was the temperature that did. Cutting across the forest would take at least an hour, maybe two, and she wasn't dressed for being outside in below-freezing weather. The only option was to call his bluff.

Securing the gun back in her belt, Hannah stepped out and watched the man closely. Standing there, she felt very helpless.

"Sorry for sneaking into your garage, but I'm looking for a particular truck. Nothing more," Hannah said.

"Sneaking? I don't know where you're from, but up in these parts we call it breaking and entering."

Hannah removed the gun and rested it against her thigh, keeping her motions slow. A test to see if he was really blind. The man didn't flinch. Either he had nerves of steel, or he was in fact telling the truth.

"I don't want to get caught up in the semantics. If you want to call the cops, you can, but I can promise you I won't be here when they arrive."

"I'm not calling the damn cops. I hate those bastards almost as much as I hate thieves."

"Good thing I'm neither," she said.

"Yeah, good thing for you, or else I'd have to try to chase you down and whack you with my cane."

Hannah smiled. "Since I'm already here, do you mind if I ask you a few questions?"

The man scratched his head for a moment. "I don't get many visitors anymore, so sure, why not? Well, there is one contingency."

"And what is that?"

"You gotta grab me a beer from that cooler over there," he said, pointing his cane at a Styrofoam cooler on the opposite side of the porch. "And grab one for yourself if you want."

Hannah placed the gun into her belt, then retrieved two Coors Lights, handing the man one. After popping open the beer, he took a long gulp, then invited her to sit at the patio table. They sat down across from each other, and as she sipped on the beer, she drew circles in the dust on the glass surface.

"Are you Richard Harrison?"

"That's the name they gave me."

The stench of alcohol was staggering; if the man had told her he bathed in beer, she wouldn't have been surprised.

"Is that your truck in the garage?" she said.

"I'm guessing you're here because it's registered to me, so you already know it is."

"I'm asking because I don't see you being able to drive it very far."

Raising his eyebrows above the rim of the sunglasses, he said, "Well honey, I haven't always been blind. All this happened about five years ago. Damn diabetes got me. Doctor says I'm close to losing my foot if I don't clean up my lifestyle," he said, making air quotes with his fingers on the final word. He took a large drink, then said, "But I've never been one to listen to doctors' orders. And on that note, would you mind getting me another one?"

Hannah grabbed the empty, tossed it in the trash can, and returned with another beer.

"When was the last time that truck was driven?" Hannah said, sliding the can across the table.

"That thing? I reckon at least a couple of years."

"So, no one has borrowed it, or anything like that?"

He chuckled. "No, no. That sucker is loud as a herd of cattle, and I'm pretty much here 24/7 so I would've heard it. It probably doesn't even start anymore. And I wouldn't be surprised if my damn ex-wife stole the battery. That wouldn't be the only thing she took from me. I'm still paying off those boobs," he said with a loud laugh.

Ignoring the comment about his ex, Hannah removed the registration and slid it across the table. "I might've accidentally removed this from your glovebox."

"Accidentally, huh?" the man said, before coughing and spitting onto the patio. "Just for shits and giggles, what type of crime are you investigating?"

After considering the question for a moment, Hannah said it plainly. "Homicide. Well, six homicides."

"No shit? A serial killer in our lovely state."

Hannah nodded, forgetting for a moment that Richard was blind. "Yeah, one that I believe lives within a twenty-five-mile radius of Laramie—and has lived here for a very long time. Probably ten years, if not longer."

Looking deep in thought, Richard took a large drink.

"How many men do you got on your list?" he said.

"Five, including you."

"Beside me, how many have you visited?"

"You're the first."

"Interesting. Do you mind if I ask who else is on it?"

Reaching into her back pocket, Hannah removed the paper, unfolded it, and read the names to Richard.

"I don't know Terry or Dennis, but I can promise you that there is no way in hell that James is your man. I've known him since high school, and we were in the service together. Hell, he was at my damn wedding. The guy is salt of the earth. And Donald, I know him a little. I worked with him for a few years down at the power plant. Quiet, nice guy, kept to himself for the most part. Dumb as a rock though, so I can't really see him as a serial killer who'd be able to avoid capture."

"That's always what a neighbor says when being interviewed by the news reporter about the killer who lived next door."

Richard chuckled. "I'm just saying if I were you, I'd start with one of the other two, rather than James or Donald."

Back in her car, Hannah stared at the paper and sucked down three consecutive cigarettes. Richard's name was crossed out, and she'd added an asterisk next to James and Donald. After the final drag, she stabbed the cigarette into the ashtray, then turned on the headlights.

At the front of the car, she cast a shadow into the trees. It stretched like a giant.

"Heads is Terry, and tails is Dennis," she said.

Meticulously, Hannah positioned a quarter on her thumb and flipped it in the air. She watched as it rotated end over end over end, countless times. As the coin fell back to earth, Hannah snatched it and slammed it onto the top of her hand.

After counting to three, she lifted her hand up, revealing the coin. It was heads. Terry.

EIGHT

Leaning against a tree, Hannah studied the house, nervously drumming her fingers on her pant leg. The moment she'd seen the house from the brush, she had a strong gut feeling that it belonged to the man she'd been searching for.

Hannah had a direct line of sight into the living room, and the black Ford F-150 parked in the driveway and the backyard patio. A man, presumably Terry, was sitting on the couch, watching TV. His gaze was perfectly aligned with Hannah, but at almost three hundred feet, she knew it was impossible for him to see her. The distance was too great, and the night was too dark, and the forest was too dense, but she still had a weird feeling that he knew she was there.

Glancing at her watch, she saw that it was 7:15. Almost forty-five minutes since she buried her car on a forest service road about a half mile from the house, and almost fifteen minutes since she arrived at her observation post. For the first ten, he hadn't moved, and Hannah thought he might be sleeping or passed out, or it could've been some sort of elaborate decoy, but he'd picked up a remote off the couch arm, then seemingly flipped a few channels before placing it in his lap, returning to his statue state.

Crawling around to the front of the tree trunk, Hannah lowered herself down, resting her back against the bark. It was sticky, with sap or resin seeping from the pores of the tree. Each time she moved, she had to peel her jacket off the bark.

In the distance, five, maybe ten miles away, a radio tower reached hundreds of feet into the sky, probably one of the tallest structures in Wyoming, broadcasting radio waves to thousands of residents, none of which could help Hannah at that very moment.

Hannah lingered for another ten minutes, watching the man. In that time, he'd only moved twice—once to pick up the remote again, and the other time to take a drink of something. It felt like he was waiting for her to make the first move.

A strong gust of wind slapped her hair into her face. Hannah turned in every direction to avoid the wind, but there was no escaping it. Temperatures were dropping, probably hovering around the thirties, and even with a winter jacket and gloves, she was freezing. She could last another hour, maybe two, but the longer she remained, the colder the night would get.

She began to grow impatient, and wanted to get a closer view, but the house was brightly lit. Plus, even though it was surrounded by forest, the field leading up to the place was completely barren. Not a tree, not a bush, not even a rock or tall grass to hide behind. She would be seen the moment she stepped out of the forest. No choice but to wait.

About twenty minutes later, the man picked up the

remote, held it for a moment, then placed it back on the arm of the couch and disappeared out of view. Hannah leaned forward and slid her palm to the handle of the gun.

Moments later, the lights in the house dimmed, and then the porch light turned on and the front door swung open. The man stood on the porch, appearing to enjoy the fresh air. He turned slowly and looked in Hannah's direction. She froze. Her first thought was that he'd somehow seen her. Maybe the gun in her lap had reflected light, or maybe the zipper on her jacket, or maybe she wasn't hidden as well as she thought, and he'd simply seen her.

After a long stare into the forest, he turned away and started walking up the driveway to the Ford F-150. He climbed in, started the truck, and put it in reverse, then turned around and drove down the long dirt road. Seconds later, the taillights disappeared, and about a minute later, the roaring engine faded into nothing. The constant hum of cicadas started, and it was oddly soothing.

"Five minutes. No, seven. No, five," Hannah whispered, her throat tightening.

Five minutes felt like the perfect length of time. If he was gone that long, he probably was heading back into town and would be gone at least twenty minutes, if not longer. That'd be enough time for her to investigate the property, the house, the rooms, and determine her next move.

She waited exactly five minutes, then looked up to the sky and whispered, "Wish me luck, Casey."

As she crept to the house, there was a metallic taste in the air, like sucking on a penny. Maybe from the brakes off a distant train, or an oil well. Whatever it was, it gave Hannah an uneasy feeling. It was what she imagined the air smelled like when Kevin Strand burned his victims in a metal drum. That was a detail she wished she'd never read, and one she could happily forget.

When she got closer to the house, her steps shortened, and she took great care with each one, fearful of potential booby traps scattered across the property. It took her twice as long as it should've to reach the perimeter of the yard.

At about forty feet away, the back porch light turned on and Hannah dropped to her stomach, gun out in front of her, prepared to fire at anyone that moved. But there wasn't anyone, and about thirty seconds later, the light turned off.

"Damn motion detector," she said.

Hannah carefully pushed off the ground, and backtracked about ten feet, then circled around the house, avoiding what she imagined was the motion detection zone. The light never turned back on.

With her back hugging the siding, Hannah made her way to the living room window, the same one she'd watched from the forest. She looked at her observation post. It was pitch dark, and visibility was probably only a hundred feet—there was no way anyone could've seen her unless they had night-vision goggles. And the odds of someone having goggles were slim, but if anyone did, it'd probably be a serial killer.

After a deep breath, Hannah placed her head next to the window and listened. Dead quiet. Then she peered through the bottom of the window into the living room. There was the couch the man had been sitting on, and a lamp that was turned on, and the TV, which was off. Nothing out of the ordinary.

After another minute of nothing, she slid her right hand through the cut in the screen and pressed on the window, but it didn't budge. Then she noticed a piece of wood in the window track that blocked it from being opened.

"Fuck," she whispered.

With extreme caution and utter silence, Hannah maneuvered across the patio to the second window on the back of the house. The window was smaller and positioned higher on the wall, so Hannah had to extend onto her tippytoes to get a glimpse into the room.

Inside, the walls were white, the bedsheet and single pillowcase were white, the headboard was white, and the carpet was an off-white. Even the dresser and nightstand were white. The only thing in the room that wasn't white was the black vintage jewelry box perfectly positioned on top of the dresser. The moment she saw the jewelry box, she knew, without a doubt what was inside.

Hannah grabbed a five-gallon bucket from under a water spigot and placed it upside down under the window. With care, she stepped on the bucket then ripped out the screen and tossed it behind her. Using both hands, she pushed up on the glass until the window was completely open. Then after a silent prayer, she pulled herself up through the window and lowered herself onto the carpet. The room smelled of lilac. Maybe a burning candle or incense. It reminded her of her grandma's house.

With her back against the wall, she remained still for a long time, gun trained on the door. Somewhere a clock ticked in a perfect rhythm like an eternal metronome. After a minute, maybe two, she inched her way to the dresser and placed her hand on the jewelry box. With eyes slightly closed and taking slow, measured breaths, she lifted the lid until it was fully open. Gingerly. she opened her left eye wide and peered down into the box.

In the top left compartment was a silver flower pendant necklace. The necklace looked identical to the one Casey had received for her high school graduation. The last time Hannah had seen it was the last time she saw her sister alive. To Hannah's knowledge, she'd worn it every day up until her death, and it was never recovered.

Hand trembling, Hannah picked up the necklace and turned it over. The engraving read "To Casey, Congrats to our brilliant daughter and loving sister. Love Mom, Dad, Hannah."

Tears began rushing down her face, and she started wheezing. She was moments from an anxiety attack, and if she didn't get it under control, she could easily faint and pass out.

Hannah took steps backward until she was at the bed, then gradually lowered herself down until she was sitting on the mattress. She brought the necklace to her lips and closed her eyes. She remained on the bed for what could've been a minute, or it could've been ten—at that moment, she had no sense of time.

Finally, she hung the necklace around her neck and tucked the pendant into her shirt, then pushed off the bed and lumbered back to the dresser. Inside the jewelry box were another four necklaces and two sets of earrings. If each piece of jewelry was a keepsake from a kill, that meant there were seven murders, not six.

Reaching for the jewelry box, Hannah grabbed the necklaces and earrings and jammed them into her front jacket pocket and zipped it up. Then she began throwing open the drawers of the dresser, searching for any other clues of the murders, but the items were what someone would expect to find from a middle-aged man: socks, underwear, T-shirts, and two full drawers of jeans.

After slamming shut the last drawer, she dropped to one knee and lifted up the bedsheet to search under the bed. Nothing—not a single item. As she let go of the bedsheet, the sound of a truck engine broke the near silence.

Like a gymnast, she sprang to her feet and darted across the floor, almost weightless. Her heart raced, making more noise than she was comfortable with. She watched as headlights bounced across the driveway. She couldn't make out the vehicle, but she knew it was Terry returning. It had to be him.

Hannah exited the room and made her way down the hallway and into the living room. She surveyed the space, searching for the perfect location for when the front door opened. Not too far, and not too close. About ten feet directly in front of the door, centered between the living room and dining room. She strategically positioned her feet, leaned into her heels, and arched her back. After wiping the sweat off her forehead, she trained the barrel of the gun at the door.

Standing there, she realized the door would open, and she'd be face-to-face with the man who'd killed her sister. Two scenarios played out in her head. One, she could instantly shoot him. No questions, no conversation, no trial or jail. He'd be dead, and Hannah would probably have to face the consequences, morally and judicially, but she would've vindicated Casey's murder. In that scenario, however, the other murders might go unsolved forever, and those families would live forever with the never-ending nightmare that had haunted Hannah for the last decade.

Two, she could hold the man at gunpoint, forcing him into restraints, be it either duct tape or rope, then call the sheriff to the house and hand over the jewelry. That should be enough evidence to arrest the man and get a search warrant for the property. Hannah had studied serial killers, and she knew odds were that he had other trophies from his kills. All the murders could be solved, and he'd spend the rest of his life rotting in a tiny jail cell, knowing it was Hannah, sister of Casey, who finally brought him to justice.

As much as she wanted to select option one and kill the man, she knew her only rational course of action was to apprehend him.

The truck came to a stop on the gravel driveway. The engine turned off, then the door slammed shut, then boots on the walkway. Her breathing intensified as she waited for the door to open. There was a long pause, and for a moment Hannah thought he could see her shadow through the living room window. As she was about to take cover behind the couch, she heard the jingling of keys. Then the deadbolt turned and the door started to creep open.

The man stepped into the hallway, holding a six-pack of Bud Light in one hand and casually resting his other hand on his thigh, with his thumb in his jean pocket. The man didn't resemble the monster Hannah had imagined. Clean clothes, groomed hair, somewhat in shape and attractive for his age. He looked like countless dads that coached little league.

With a bloodless glare, the man didn't take an eye off Hannah. He just reached back and closed the door casually, almost like he was concerned about letting cold air into the house.

"Get on the fucking ground," she said, emphasizing each word.

The man didn't respond. Not a word, not a facial expression. Nothing. He was completely still except for occasionally blinking, and even that felt like it came at extended intervals.

The distance between them was a little too close for her comfort. She was almost certain it'd take at least four seconds to cover the ground, and in that time, she could get off at least two rounds, but that didn't ease her nerves. All she wanted was to take four steps back, but she couldn't appear apprehensive.

Leisurely, the man knelt and placed the six-pack on the floor, then pulled a bottle out of the cardboard container and stood back up. He twisted off the cap and dropped it at his feet. The cap bounced twice before coming to a rest next to his boot.

Bringing the beer bottle to his lips, he tilted it back, and with his eyes closed, took a long, slow drink. His demeanor was more that of someone at a Labor Day barbecue than someone with the barrel of a gun pointed at them.

He puckered his lips. "I knew I'd see you again, but I'd be lying if I thought it was going to be in my own living room."

Cutting him off, Hannah said, "Shut up and get on the floor!"

With every ounce of strength, she tried to hold the gun steady, but the barrel was starting to waver. She cleared her throat and tried to sound strong, but as she spoke, her voice cracked like that of a prepubescent boy. "I swear I'm not going to say it again."

From under the coffee table, a calico cat appeared. It pranced toward Hannah, bunting against her legs.

"I call her Mittens. She was a stray that appeared on my door step about a year ago, severely malnourished. I fed her once and she hasn't left since," the man said, like he was talking to a neighbor.

Hannah grinned and let out a small chuckle. It wasn't that she thought the situation was humorous. It was the anxiety that always brought out an awkward laughter. When she was nervous, she laughed. When she had a class presentation, she laughed. When she didn't know what to say to someone, she laughed. And when she feared for her life, she laughed.

Choosing her words carefully, Hannah said, "I know you killed my sister. Along with all those other girls.

And I can promise that you'll never hurt another girl again."

Hannah locked her elbows and extended the gun. The man didn't move, didn't say anything. He remained completely still. That terrified her.

With heavy feet, she took two steps forward. "I said get on the fucking ground!"

He turned his head to the left, held it there for a moment, then jerked it to the right, cracking what sounded like every vertebrae in his neck. For almost a minute, neither of them spoke.

Then, with a hint of a grin, he said, "I've been watching and waiting for you, Hannah. Waiting for the next crescent moon."

"I don't care about any of the nonsense that comes out of your mouth. I swear I'll put a bullet in your fucking head," she said. "This is your last warning."

"If you were going to shoot me, you would've done it the moment I stepped in the door," he said.

In the four years since she'd carried a firearm, she'd pointed the barrel at a total of three people. Three. The man who fled from Las Vegas after skipping out on bail for a second-degree burglary charge—she couldn't remember his name. Then there was the night when someone attempted to mug her in the alley behind her apartment in Capitol Hill. She barely had the gun out of her purse before the man turned and ran faster than Carl Lewis. Probably a drug addict looking for an easy score. Little did he know. Then there was the night in the park when Tom caught Nathan Cook, but that wasn't even her gun. It was Tom's.

On all three of those occasions, she never intended to pull the trigger. Never. It was more of a way to take control of the situation and protect herself from getting injured or killed, but this was different. She wanted this man dead, and she wanted him to suffer. And even though the man had killed Casey, and Julia, and probably at least five other women, and would likely kill again, she was apprehensive. Killing another human was something that she'd never thought she'd have to consider. She wasn't sure how she'd be able to live after taking another life.

Hannah ordered him to the ground again, louder this time.

With thin eyes, the man gave her a blank stare. "You shouldn't have come here."

The room seemed to become darker, but Hannah knew that was impossible—neither of them had moved. Maybe it was something trying to protect her from her imminent fate. The longer he stood still like a statue, the more her confidence waned, and the certainty that she'd never walk out of the house became more of a reality.

The man kicked the bottle cap, and it landed about halfway between them. As she watched it bounce across the floor, she got a feeling that everything was about to go wrong.

With his left eyebrow cocked, he said, "You made a big mistake coming here. All you had to do was get in your car and drive back to your nice little apartment in Capitol Hill, and since I don't particularly enjoy Denver, I might've left you alone. But you had to come to Laramie, and you had to snoop around, and to make matters worse, you arrive at my house, my sanctuary, unannounced."

"Get on the fucking ground!" she screamed.

From somewhere very deep inside of her, something said pull the trigger, and just as she was about to fire the gun, the man released the beer bottle. Almost in slow motion, Hannah watched as it slipped from his hand and crash to the hardwood floor, shattering into hundreds of tiny glass shards. And while the bottle was in free fall, he reached to his back, and in a near-single motion he extracted a knife out from a holder and flung it at Hannah.

It was a blur, happening in milliseconds, but Hannah saw the blade hurling through the air toward her. There was no time to react, no time to move, no time to gasp, no time to do anything. The knife hit her left thigh, and for a moment she was unsure if it had cut into her flesh or the handle had hit her thigh and bounced off, and she was too scared to look.

As the man escaped into another room, Hannah fired two rounds, one hitting the door and another the wall of the room he'd gone into. He never even looked back. She heard him knock over some plates, then run down a set of stairs. Maybe a root cellar, maybe a torture room.

Hastily, Hannah glanced down at her leg, and finally saw the knife protruding out of her left thigh, about three inches below her hip. Judging by the size of the handle, her guess was that the blade was probably at least four or five inches. Remarkably, she didn't feel the knife or any type of pain from the laceration, but she presumed that was due to an adrenaline spike. It would only be a matter of time before the pain set in.

Not wanting to be in the same location if the man returned, Hannah limped into the dining room, then pulled out two chairs and placed them on either side of her, creating a makeshift barrier. She leaned into the corner and slowly lowered herself to the ground. Once on the floor, she placed the gun on top of the chair, pointing the barrel toward the living room. She felt somewhat safe—well, as safe as she could given the circumstances. There was no way that he could sneak up behind her, and she had a view of both the living room and kitchen.

Her forehead was drenched, as well as her shirt, and

there was about a three-inch-diameter spot in her jeans that was turning dark red, as well as a pool of blood collecting on the hardwood floor under her leg. The nausea kicked in, and her throat became drier than she'd ever experienced, like being dehydrated and without water in Death Valley. She would've given anything for a sip of water.

If she'd been anywhere else but Terry's house, she probably would've succumbed to the pain and passed out, but she knew if she did, she'd be raped and murdered, and probably never found. He'd dispose of her body in the basement or in the endless forest behind the house.

Sooner or later, her dad or Doug would go looking for her, but that might take a week or two, and by that point, the motel room would've been cleaned and any valuables would've been taken by the housekeeping staff, and everything else would've been tossed into the dumpster and buried deep into a landfill. There'd be no clues. Nobody would know what happened to her, and she'd become another girl who'd never be found. Another statistic for the missing person tally.

Stay awake, stay awake. Breathe. One one thousand, two one thousand, three one thousand. Breathe, breathe, breathe.

Her most pressing concern wasn't the killer in the house, it was the knife in her upper thigh. Her biggest fear was that it had hit the femoral artery, and if she pulled it out, she knew she'd bleed to death in mere minutes, but she also realized that it'd be impossible to fight the man with the handle of a knife protruding out of her leg, and if she couldn't detain the man, she was as good as dead anyway.

Hannah thought back to a first-aid training Marshall required her to take. It was advised not to remove embedded objects, but that wasn't an option, so the next viable steps were to control and, if possible, stop the bleeding. Once the bleeding was under control, it was crucial to apply dressing to the wound.

Reaching to the table, she grabbed a hand towel. Then using all her might, she pulled it around her thigh above the knife. Her leg pulsated around the blade, but it strangely felt warm, somewhat soothing. Maybe her body was trying to mask the pain.

Turning her head, she bit down hard on her jacket sleeve, then wrapped her hand around the knife handle. *Like a Band-Aid, fast and swift.*

With her eyes closed, she took three deep breaths, in through the nose, out through the mouth. Then after the third exhale, she yanked the knife out of her thigh.

She expected her leg to resemble a water fountain after the blade was removed, but following a quick burst of blood, the stream began to lessen to a trickle. Hannah let out a quick sigh, realizing the blade had missed her femoral artery. She jammed the knife into the floor, then ripped off the tablecloth and pressed it as hard as she could on the wound, holding it there for about two minutes.

Her muscles were tense, her breathing was labored, and her heart hammered against her chest. There was a sharp pain in her toes on the injured leg, and she wasn't sure if that was normal for a stabbing, or if it was critical and needed immediate medical attention. Better not to think about it. With her hands resting on her chest, Hannah leaned her head back and focused on her breathing. After what felt like minutes, her pulse lowered, and she finally caught her breath.

While Hannah was tending to her wound, the house grew silent. There were some footsteps, and the slamming of a door in the basement, but nothing that sounded like it was a threat to Hannah. And for the final minute of her first-aid care, there wasn't a sound. She wondered if he escaped the house, but something told her he'd never run from her.

She began surveying the house and saw a phone on the counter in the kitchen. In all likelihood, the man had already disconnected or cut the phone lines, but Hannah had to attempt to call 911. If the phone worked, it'd be a chance for survival, and if it didn't—well, that was something she didn't want to think about.

Hannah clambered to her feet, then took a moment to gather her balance before trudging into the kitchen. The longer she stood on her leg, the more intense the pain became. Maybe it was the adrenaline starting to wean.

Stretching across the counter, Hannah grabbed the phone and put the headset to her ear. Nothing. The line was dead. Frantically, she pressed the hook switch about ten times in five seconds, but it was still dead. She stared at the phone for a moment, then gently placed the headset down onto the receiver.

Easing to the sink, she picked up a dirty glass and filled it up, then chugged it in one drink. She filled it up two more times, then placed the glass back into the sink. With the faucet still on, she started splashing water onto her face, then dried her face with a washcloth and turned off the water.

As she turned back to the living room, the sound of "Cherry Cherry" by Neil Diamond blared throughout the house. The music was deafening. With her free hand, Hannah covered her left ear in an attempt to deaden the noise, but the attempt was futile.

"I'm going to kill you, you fucking son of a bitch!" Hannah screamed, knowing that he couldn't hear her. She could barely hear herself.

Out of the corner of her eye, Hannah spotted a speaker

on top of the microwave. Leaning over the counter, she grabbed the speaker and yanked out the wires, but there was no change in the volume of the music. There were probably dozens of speakers strategically placed throughout the house, and she'd probably have to destroy half of them to decrease the volume. Hannah tossed the speaker at the refrigerator, and it bounced off and landed hard on the tile, coming within inches of slamming back into her right shin.

A quick glance over her shoulder back to the dining room, then she made her way to the stairway and looked down the narrow, rickety steps. The only light shone from the kitchen, and about halfway down, the light disappeared. Everything beyond that was complete darkness. There wasn't a railing, and the stairs were uneven, different heights and different lengths. Even uninjured, the odds of tripping were high. There was no way she'd attempt to maneuver them on one leg.

The music was distracting; her thoughts were incoherent. He was playing mental games and winning. Probably baiting her to go down the stairs, waiting in the dark for her. He could jump out of the shadows below and fire a gun before she'd have time to react, but then she remembered that all the murders were strangulations or with a knife. He preferred killing with his hands, and if he was going to kill Hannah, it wouldn't be with a firearm. That wasn't intimate enough for him.

After screaming some more obscenities, she lowered the gun and fired one round into the basement. The muzzle flash lit up the stairwell for an instant, and the bullet ricocheted off the cement and disappeared into the darkness.

Stumbling through the kitchen, Hannah returned to the dining room. Walking was becoming difficult, and as she reached the table, her legs began to quiver. Her body felt like she'd completed a ten-mile hike with a two-thousand-foot elevation gain, not a simple walk from room to room. She wasn't sure how much longer she could keep moving. Hell, she wasn't even sure how much longer she could stand.

The pain was becoming unbearable—she was on the verge of passing out. As much as she wanted to sit and rest for a minute or two, she knew that wasn't an option, because she might not be able to get back up. It had been about ten minutes since she removed the knife, and her leg was still bleeding. There was a trail of blood behind her like she was an animal that'd been struck on a highway. Between the blood on the floor and the stains on her clothes, she'd probably lost at least a pint, and she prayed it wasn't much more than that. Four pints was critical blood loss. At that point, her blood pressure would plummet, and her organs would begin to fail. And within minutes, she'd pass out and die. *Four pints.*

She briefly considered trekking back to her car, but she'd almost twisted her ankle three times on the way to the house, so it'd be impossible to make the journey now. Then she thought about attempting to make her way down the driveway to the county road, but it was at least a half mile, and likely frequented more by animals than vehicles. It'd also leave her completely exposed. Nope, she was trapped in the house with Terry, and the chances of her escaping were becoming slim.

"You fucking coward! Come out and fight!" she screamed, barely able to hear herself over the music.

Seconds later, the song ended, and the house became quiet, like being in the eye of a hurricane. The only sounds were her gasping breaths and the rattling of the furnace. A subtle ringing filled her ears, and with her index finger, she attempted to massage her ear canal, but it did nothing. The ringing continued.

As she made her way into the living room, the floorboard creaked under her shoes, and as she approached the couch, she heard a loud thump from behind. She whirled around, gun drawn, moments from firing, but it was only the cat jumping off the kitchen table and onto the floor. It looked at Hannah, then scurried past her into the hallway and out of sight.

Just as Hannah was becoming accustomed to the silence, "Cherry Cherry" restarted, echoing throughout the house again, seemingly louder. Hannah screamed, then turned and stared into the TV's reflection, her thoughts in disarray.

She never heard the footsteps, but she felt the ground shake like a grizzly bear running down its prey. There was no time to turn around and get off a shot. There wasn't even enough time to jump out of harm's way. Maybe if she'd had another few feet, but she didn't, and for a split-second time stood still.

With the man almost on top of her, she dropped to the floor like a ragdoll. Tucking her head into her knees, she tried to make herself as small a target as possible. And just as she was about to turn toward him, his shins collided with Hannah's ribcage, flipping her onto her back, and when she landed, she lost her grip of the gun and it clattered across the floor, coming to a rest about five feet out of reach.

Terry tripped over Hannah and tumbled into the coffee table, knocking it over and launching everything on top of it into the air, including two large pillar candles. Both candles landed on the area rug then rolled across the floor before coming to a rest under the drapes.

When the man slammed into the ground, the floor rattled like a small tremor. There was a loud crack as he landed, and Hannah wasn't sure if he'd broken something or if it was from the music, or something in her imagination.

Hannah glanced at the man. He was unresponsive. Maybe he'd knocked himself out when he collided with the hardwood, a concussion or a skull fracture, or maybe, hopefully, he'd broken his neck and was dead.

Taking her eyes off of him, she focused on the gun in front of her. It was only a couple of feet away, but it felt like a hundred. Right then, she decided that if she could reach the gun, she'd fire every remaining bullet into his worthless body.

Before she could move, there was a loud grunt, and when she looked back, Terry was on his feet. Like a drunk, he was swaying, and his right arm hung lower than his left. Maybe a dislocated shoulder or broken collarbone. If he was in pain, he didn't show it.

"I'm going to make you pay for this, you little bitch," he said, exhaling heavily out of his nostrils.

Hannah turned and started crawling on her hands and knees to the gun. Five feet. Four feet. His footsteps were close. Three feet. Two feet. With her right arm stretched out, she could feel his presence on top of her.

Her hand was inches from the gun when she felt a tug on her jacket. She clawed her fingernails into the floor, but it was to no avail. Terry lifted her up a few feet, then hurled her to the ground.

She hit the floor hard, nearly getting the wind knocked out of her. Before she could think, he grabbed the back of the jacket and started pulling her toward him, away from the gun. After a few seconds, he flipped her onto her back and hovered over her.

"Look at me! Look at me!" the man screamed like a rabid dog.

Hannah turned away from him. If he was going to kill her, she wasn't going to give him the satisfaction of obeying his demands.

"I said look at me," he said, this time in a calm, calculated voice.

Looking past the couch, past the coffee table, past the entertainment center, Hannah saw that the candles had ignited the tassel fringe at the bottom of the drapes. It would only be a matter of moments before they were engulfed in flames. Staring at the fire, she crafted her escape plan.

"Take a look," Hannah said, gesturing toward the window with her head.

Terry kept his eyes on Hannah in a long stare, then slowly tilted his head. Confusion came over his face.

"What the fuck?" he said.

"I hope you burn in hell," she whispered.

With all the strength she had remaining, she brought her good leg back and propelled it forward, square into his groin. For a moment, he stood still, unmoved. Then the color left his face, and he faltered back a few steps until his legs gave out and he fell to the floor, missing Hannah by about six inches.

Without hesitation, Hannah propelled herself off the ground and started toward the gun. Again, Terry grabbed her jacket, but this time, she was prepared. Reaching for the zipper, she yanked it down and slid out of the sleeves in one-continuous motion, leaving the man holding the jacket in the air.

She picked up the gun and turned around. They stared at each other for only a second or two, and then he looked away, conceding to her. And as Hannah watched the final moments of his life, she felt an unspoken word pass between them. Maybe it was his soul preparing to leave his body. Maybe it was what someone felt when taking another person's life.

"This is for Casey."

Terry held up the jacket as to shield himself, but nothing could protect him from his impending demise. With a steady hand, Hannah pulled the trigger, firing one round. The bullet struck him in the lower abdomen, and he bellowed, crying out as tears began cascading down his cheeks.

As she watched the man thrash on the floor, a morbid pleasure overcome her—she knew that the abdomen was one of the most painful places to get shot. Stomach acids and bile would leak into the body and spread to other organs. His last remaining moments on earth would be slow and agonizing.

In one final attempt to capture Hannah, Terry lunged toward her, but she was prepared, taking a step back and out of his reach. The man fell to his elbows and let out a heavy sigh, then with fear in his eyes, he rolled away and onto the jacket. A final resting spot. Hannah raised the gun and fired two more rounds into his back.

For almost a minute, Hannah watched the man, never looking away. He didn't move, and it didn't appear as if he was breathing. She was certain that he was dead.

Shifting her gaze across the room, Hannah saw that the curtains were now an inferno, and even though she was twenty feet away, the heat was stifling. Soon the house would be fully engulfed in flames, everything within its walls incinerated—her included if she didn't leave now.

Hannah hobbled out of the house, crossed the walkway, and made it to the driveway, then leaned onto the truck to rest. Glancing back, she remembered the jewelry she placed in the jacket pocket.

"Fuck!" she screamed.

Briefly she considered going back inside and seizing the jacket out of the man's hands, but the fire had spread to the walls and ceiling, and the entire house was mere minutes from collapsing on itself in a pile of flames and ashes. There was no way she'd be able to retrieve the jacket and make it out alive, especially with one bad leg.

After gathering some strength, Hannah turned away from the house and continued toward the road. The wind was strong, and the flames felt like they were getting hotter even as she distanced herself. The pain was agonizing, and she stumbled as she walked, unsure how much she could continue. But she didn't stop. Each time she nearly fell, she gathered strength and held herself up.

Halfway up the driveway, Hannah spotted emergency lights on the horizon. They looked to be about a mile away. Someone must've seen the fire or heard the gunshots and called 911. Rescue was en route, and a sense a relief overcame her.

Seconds later, there was an explosion, and when Hannah turned around, the house burst into a fireball. The shockwave knocked her to the gravel. Glass, wood, and brick rained down through the air. She covered her head with one arm, trying to protect herself from any debris.

As the sirens grew louder, she closed her eyes, finally succumbing to the pain.

Three days later, Hannah was sitting up in a hospital bed, her leg heavily bandaged. The knife wound had required fourteen stitches, and she'd suffered a minor concussion from either getting knocked to the ground by the blast or when Terry knocked her over. Her ribs were bruised, and she was sore in muscles she hadn't known existed, but she was alive, and she was going to walk out of the hospital in mere hours. Within a week or two, she'd be completely healed.

The doctor had told her she was "extremely lucky"—the knife had missed her femoral artery by half an inch. She'd lost a little over two pints of blood; another two pints and she could've bled out. All facts she already knew.

"Another hour or two and you wouldn't be here. You'd be down in the morgue," the doctor had said.

Another fact she knew.

On the ambulance ride to the hospital, Hannah had never let go of the necklace. And while she was on the operating table under local anesthesia, she wouldn't let the hospital staff take it from her. Every night she'd fall asleep with it on her chest, and every morning she kissed it when she awoke. Sometime in the middle of the night, on the first night in the hospital, she made a promise to herself that she'd never let the necklace out of her grasp again. Never.

The fire made the front page of the *Laramie Tribune*. It felt like one of the biggest stories of the year in Laramie, maybe in all of Wyoming. The article stated that it took three different fire departments, with over forty firefighters, ten hours to completely extinguish the inferno. The Albany County fire chief was quoted as saying it was an ongoing investigation and he couldn't discuss the cause of the fire, and couldn't comment if there were any casualties, but he did state that there was an unconscious, unnamed female on the property, as well as a cat about a half mile away, found hiding in a hollowed-out tree. The story provided no facts she didn't already know, and there was no mention of Terry or a possible link to the unsolved murders. It didn't have to—she knew Terry was dead, and she didn't regret killing him.

Hannah tossed the paper onto the bedside table and took a bite of the hospital ham sandwich. As she choked down the meal, a soft knock came on the door. Rick was standing in the doorway.

"Mind if I come in for a couple minutes?" Rick said.

She nodded, trying to avoid his gaze.

"How's the leg?" he said.

"It's fine, but I'm guessing I won't be doing any marathons anytime soon."

"Did you run them before?"

She shook her head. "Nope, I never have."

Rick smiled, then shuffled across the tile to sit in a chair at the foot of the bed.

"What happened at the house?" he said.

Hannah let the quiet build in the room for a while. Then she shrugged and pointed at the paper. "It looks like it caught on fire."

"Quit bullshitting me, Hannah. You know exactly what I'm talking about. What were you doing there? How did you get stabbed? What happened to Terry? And how did the damn house catch on fire?"

She'd already decided she'd never tell the details of that night to another person. It'd be another secret she'd take to the grave.

Rick stared at Hannah, waiting for an answer, and she just stared at the clock on the wall, second-guessing her decision to let him into the room. Then, without saying a word, Hannah took off Casey's necklace and dangled the pendant in front of him.

"What's that?" Rick said.

Hannah turned the pendant over, then leaned in toward the sheriff.

He read the inscription aloud, then said, "I'm guessing this is your sister's necklace."

Leaning back into the bed, Hannah draped the necklace around her neck, positioning it in the middle of her chest, perfectly aligned.

"It is, and I found it in a jewelry box inside Terry's bedroom, along with six other pieces of jewelry that I suspect belonged to other murder victims."

Rick straightened up. "Where are they?"

Hannah sighed. "They were in my jacket pocket, but I lost it in the house. Hopefully they'll be found in the rubble."

"I don't think that's going to happen. There's nothing left—no house, no truck, nothing. Just a ten-foot-deep crater where the house once stood. It's like a small Hiroshima. The fire marshal said he's never seen an explosion that catastrophic in his twenty years. It'll be weeks, maybe months, until the official investigation is over, but between you and me, he suspects there might've been a box of dynamite in the house, and that might've ignited the propane tank, then boom." He paused to take a breath. "You're lucky you escaped when you did. A few minutes later, and we might not be having this conversation."

Again, someone telling her she was lucky to be alive.

"So, you haven't found Terry's body?"

Rick shook his head. "Nope. There are some forensic scientists combing through the debris, but they haven't found anything. I also have about twenty men searching a two-mile radius around the blast site, and all they've found is charred wood, broken glass, and ash. In my opinion, I highly doubt anything of significance will ever be recovered."

Hannah cursed under her breath. "What about my sister's murder? Or all the other girls?"

With defeat in his face, he shrugged. "I'll continue to

investigate the cases, but without a body, or DNA, or any evidence that links Terry to the murders, I don't foresee any developments. Come on, it's been a decade since your sister's murder—he could've obtained that necklace countless ways. Maybe he won it in a poker game."

"We both know he killed Casey, and Julia, and Alice, and Denise, and Judy and Diana, and probably more. And if you don't see that, you're a bigger moron than I thought."

Rick smiled. "Like I said, Casey and Julia are an open investigation in Albany County, and my department will continue working those cases. And I'll contact you if, and when, we have any new leads." He coughed. "Unofficially, I do think he was involved in Casey's murder, but what the hell am I supposed to do? Take that necklace to the DA office and ask him to bring murder charges against a dead man? He'd throw me in the mental ward. I really wish I could do more, I'm sorry."

As Rick was making his way out of the room, he stopped in the doorway and turned back. "Oh, I thought you might like to hear that Earl has been suspended indefinitely. He pulled over the daughter of a congressman and got a little too rough with her. The congressman made a few calls, and I suspect the 'indefinitely' will eventually become fired, so you won't have to worry about him any longer."

Unsure how to respond, Hannah just gave him a blank stare.

He waited a moment, then said, "Want me to shut this?"

After a steady nod, she watched as Rick exited the room. If she never saw him again, she'd be fine. In fact, she'd be fine if she never stepped foot in Laramie for the rest of her life.

Back in the motel room, Hannah sat on the bed, sipping on a whiskey and water. In less than two weeks, she'd found the man who had given her nightmares for over a decade. She wondered if she'd still have nightmares, and if so, what they would be.

The memory of her sister was finally at rest, and she could move forward with her life, whatever that might be. She still had nearly all of the $25,000 that Tom had given her for solving the Megan Floyd disappearance. Maybe she'd move to Cabo San Lucas, rent a villa and get drunk every day on the beach and forget about the world for a year or two.

After the final sips, Hannah dropped the plastic glass in the trash can, then picked up her bag and hobbled to the door. Out on the walkway, the sun hung low on the horizon, and in the distance, she could see a herd of pronghorn chasing the dying light.

Hannah veered to her left and found Mark leaning over the railing, smoking a cigarette. She gave a half wave.

"Howdy, stranger. How's the research paper going?" he said.

"Better than I thought."

"That's good to hear," he said, taking a drag. "I haven't seen you around in a while. Where have you been?"

"Umm, I'm guessing you don't watch the news or read the paper?"

"Nah, that shit will rot your mind. I prefer spending my free time with the likes of McCarthy, Hemingway, Fitzgerald. You ever read any of their stuff?"

"In high school, I once read Blood Meridian, but I probably only comprehended about half of it. Since then, I haven't read much."

"And why is that?"

Hannah thought for a second. "I don't know. I guess I probably should start again, though."

"Yeah, you really should. I could give you some very good recommendations if you need any."

A moment of silence followed, but not an awkward moment. A moment of tranquility. It was a feeling that she hadn't truly felt since Casey was alive. It felt good.

"So, I normally don't do this, but would you like to grab a drink and maybe something to eat? I'm starving," Hannah said.

Mark took a drag, then dropped the cigarette onto the walkway and smashed it with his boot. "Yes, that sounds amazing. Let me grab my coat."

Hannah smiled as she watched him disappear into the room. For the first time in a long time, she felt like her life was worth living, and that gave her a gleam of hope.